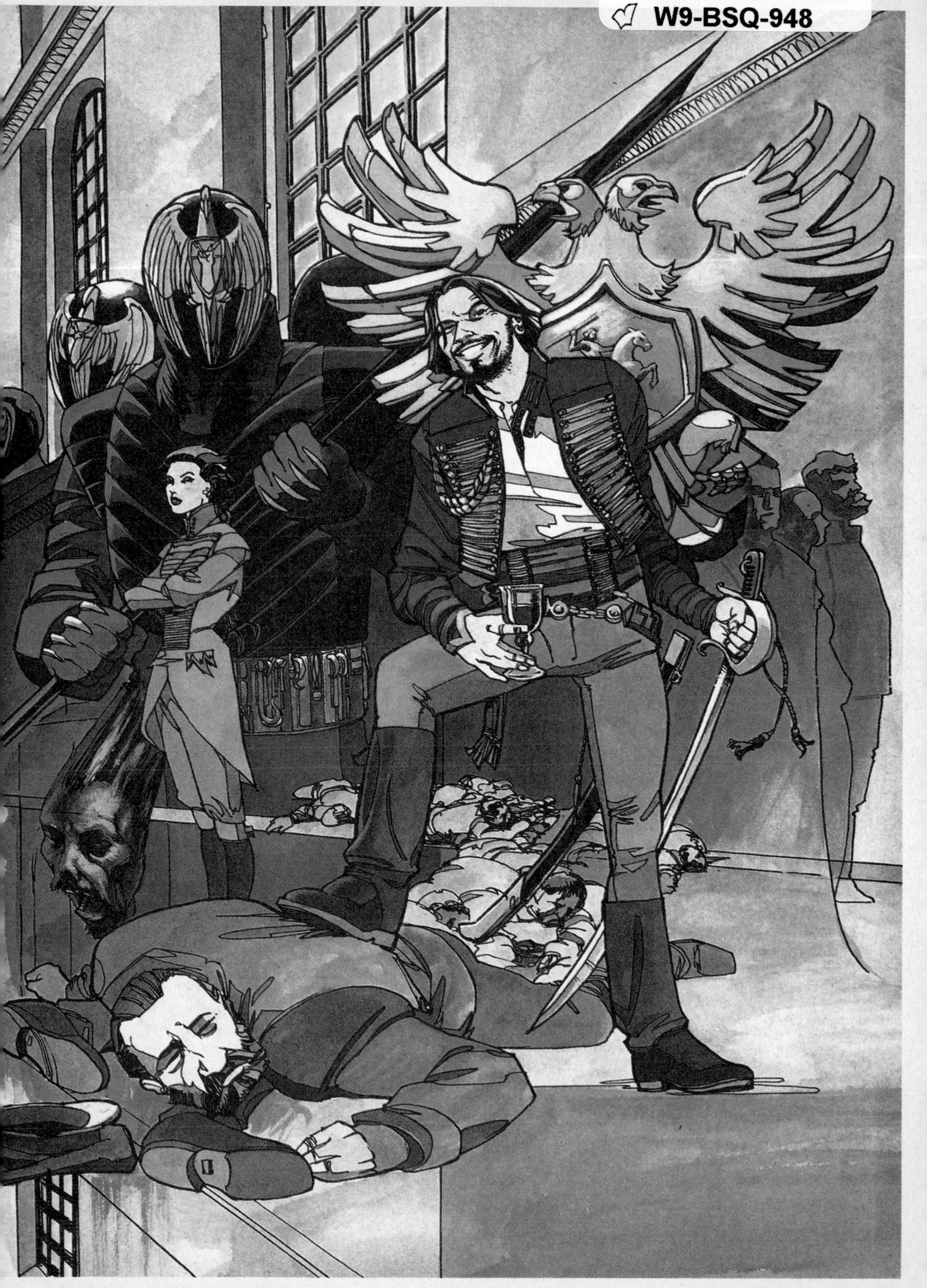

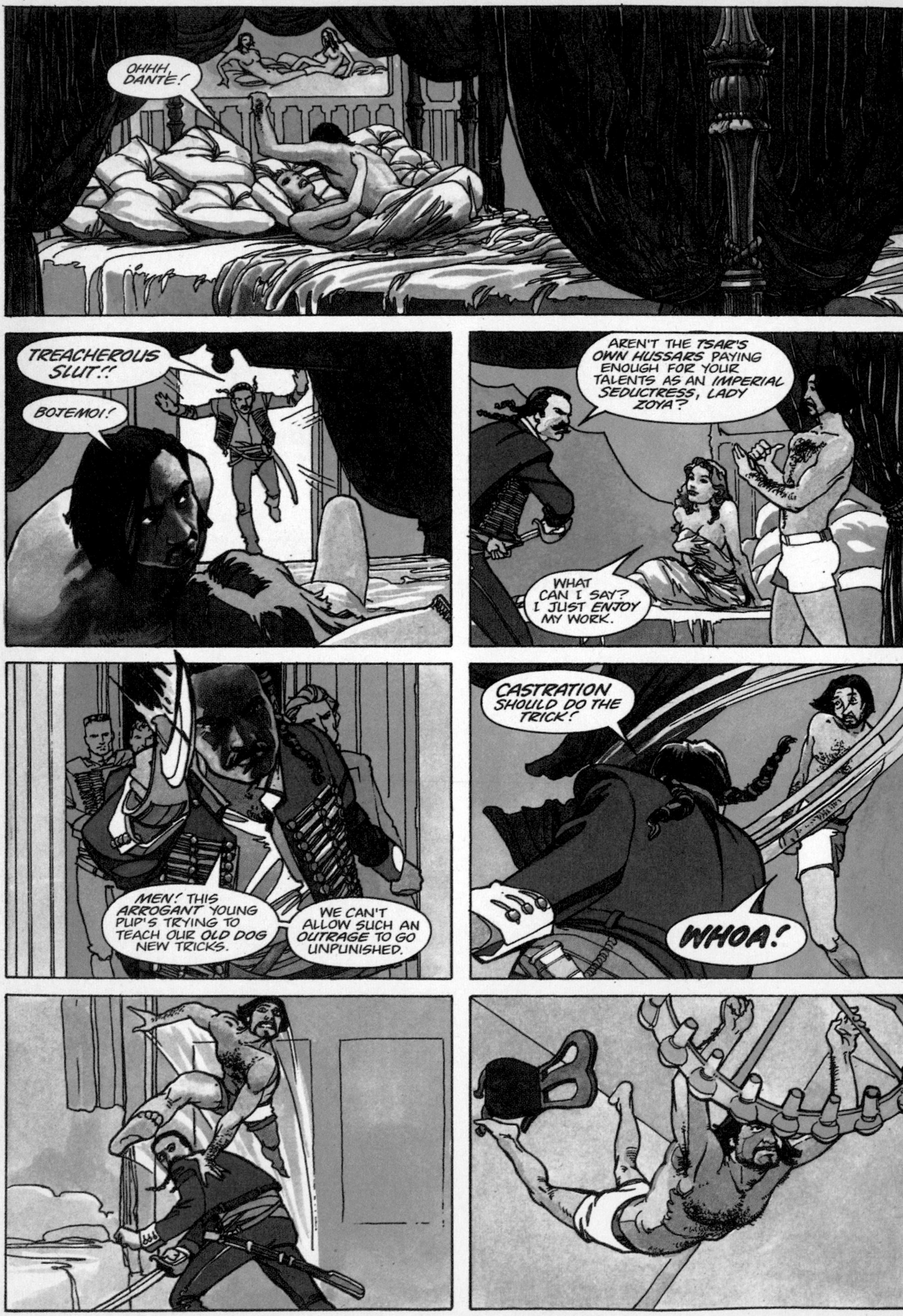
OHHH, DANTE!
TREACHEROUS SLUT!!
BOJEMOI!
AREN'T THE TSAR'S OWN HUSSARS PAYING ENOUGH FOR YOUR TALENTS AS AN IMPERIAL SEDUCTRESS, LADY ZOYA?
WHAT CAN I SAY? I JUST ENJOY MY WORK.
MEN! THIS ARROGANT YOUNG PUP'S TRYING TO TEACH OUR OLD DOG NEW TRICKS.
WE CAN'T ALLOW SUCH AN OUTRAGE TO GO UNPUNISHED.
CASTRATION SHOULD DO THE TRICK!
WHOA!

FIGHT, THIEF!

GO FOR YOUR SWORD INSTEAD OF TRAPPING MY MEN OUTSIDE!

AT LEAST DIE WITH A LITTLE HONOUR!

HONOUR BE DAMNED!!

WHY DIDN'T YOU TELL ME YOU WERE AN IMPERIAL SEDUCTRESS?

THE DANGER MAKES THE EXPERIENCE ALL THE MORE STIMULATING, WOULDN'T YOU AGREE?

SORRY TO LOVE YOU AND LEAVE YOU, LADY ZOYA.

THAT'S JUST LIFE...

MY LIFE!

THIS ISN'T MINE!

MANY THANKS, MILADY!

I'LL KEEP THIS! TREASURE IT FOREVER AS A MEMENTO OF OUR PASSION!

TSYGANOV BLACK MARKET, ST. PETERSBURG.

SEVEN HUNDRED AND FIFTY?!?

LOOK AT THOSE JEWELS. IT'S THE GENUINE ARTICLE—THE EROTICOSTUME OF AN IMPERIAL SEDUCTRESS!

A MAN OF YOUR WORLDLY WISDOM AND *SOPHISTICATION* MUST REALISE THAT.

ALRIGHT! A THOUSAND! AND THAT'S MY *LAST* OFFER...

DONE!

AND I KNOW JUST HOW TO START SPENDING IT...

MILADY!

A WOMAN OF YOUR DISTINCTION SHOULDN'T BE WANDERING THE BLACK MARKET WITHOUT AN ESCORT.

NIKOLAI DANTE! AT YOUR SERVICE.

ANY SERVICE...

BE STILL, MY THUNDERING HEART.

COMMANDER PYRE OF THE SCARLET WRAITHS. CHARMED, I'M SURE.

I SERVE THE TSAR, AND THE TSAR WISHES *YOUR HEAD!*

9

NEXT PROG ▷ TSAR WARS!

Nikolai Dante

PART 2

RUSSIA, 2666. THIS VAST NATION IS RULED BY IMPERIAL DYNASTIES, LED BY TSAR VLADIMIR THE CONQUEROR.

WHEN ROGUE NIKOLAI DANTE IS FOUND WITH AN IMPERIAL SEDUCTRESS, HE IS HUNTED BY THE TSAR'S TROOPS...

BOJEMOI!

THIS LOWBORN SWINE—THIS IS THE THIEF WHO DEFEATED CAPTAIN ARBATOV AND A *SQUAD* OF HUSSARS?

HARD TO BELIEVE, ISN'T IT?

DO YOU WISH ME TO BEAT HIM *FURTHER*, TSARINA?

TSARINA...YOU'RE JENA, THE TSAR'S *DAUGHTER?*

I'M SURPRISED A WOMAN OF YOUR POWER AND BEAUTY NEEDS SUCH CRUDE METHODS TO FIND YOURSELF A MAN.

I CONDUCT MY OWN BEATINGS, COMMANDER PYRE.

SCRIPT
ROBBIE MORRISON

ART
SIMON FRASER

LETTERS
ANNIE PARKHOUSE

THE IMPERIAL PALACE, ST. PETERSBURG.

TAKE YOUR TIME WITH HIM, MONGOLIAN...

A LITTLE BLOODSPORT ALWAYS LIVENS UP DUNGEON LIFE.

YOU'LL NOT BE SO PRETTY, BOY, WHEN I DANCE ON YOUR FACE...

I'M NOT A DANCING MAN!

OUFFF!

GNNGF!

PRISONER NIKOLAI DANTE. YOUR TIME HAS COME.

ONE SECOND, PLEASE. I JUST HAVE TO COLLECT MY WINNINGS.

11

YOU WOULDN'T BE ADVERSE TO A LITTLE *BRIBERY*, WOULD YOU?

WHAT HAVE YOU GOT TO OFFER, *THIEF*?

TWO *CIGAR-BUTTS*, A *THIMBLEFUL* OF *VODKA* AND SOMETHING THAT SMELLS *SUSPICIOUSLY* LIKE CHEESE.

YOU FOUGHT THE *MONGOLIAN* FOR SUCH *PETTY SPOILS*!?

I'M A GAMBLING MAN. OLD HABITS DIE HARD.

BESIDES, THERE'S A LIMIT TO WHAT INMATES CAN CONCEAL IN THEIR PRISON PANTS.

WELL...

MOST INMATES...

THE COURT OF *VLADIMIR THE CONQUEROR*, TSAR OF ALL THE RUSSIAS, IS NOW IN SESSION.

PRISONERS! DO NOT WEEP OR BEG. UNDIGNIFIED SIGNS OF WEAKNESS OR REPENTANCE WILL RESULT ONLY IN *HARSHER* PUNISHMENT.

NIKOLAI DANTE! PREPARE TO FACE THE JUDGEMENT OF THE TSAR.

YOU MAY BEGIN, TSAR VLADIMIR.

I'M READY TO CONDUCT MY DEFENCE.

YOU *HAVE* NO DEFENCE, BOY.

NIKOLAI DANTE, SINCE ENTERING ST. PETERSBURG RELIABLE WITNESSES HAVE CONFIRMED YOUR *GUILT* IN THE FOLLOWING CRIMES—

BANDITRY, FRAUD, DECEIT, UNAUTHORISED DUELLING AND *SEDUCTION* FOR THE PURPOSES OF FINANCIAL GAIN.

THESE LAST CHARGES ARE... *INTERESTING.*

AN ASSAULT ON A *CAPTAIN ARBATOV...* AND A COMPLAINT FROM AN *IMPERIAL SEDUCTRESS—* YOU *STOLE* HER *UNDERWEAR.*

THEY WERE A *GIFT,* IN APPRECIATION OF *SERVICES* RENDERED!

I DON'T RESORT TO THIEVERY FOR ITEMS OF SUCH *INTIMATE* APPAREL — THEY'RE *HURLED* AT ME WITH GREAT *ABANDON.*

THESE CRIMES WERE ALL COMMITTED AGAINST *RANKING* MEMBERS OF THE IMPERIAL *NOBILITY?*

THERE'S NO *FUN* OR *PROFIT* IN THIEVING FROM THOSE WHO CAN'T AFFORD IT...

THAT'S THE *WAY* OF THE *EMPIRE,* YOUNG DANTE.

IF YOU CAN'T ACCEPT THAT, YOU DON'T *DESERVE* TO LIVE AS PART OF IT.

AND THAT IS THE PENALTY FOR OFFENCES AS *GRAVE* AS YOURS...

EXECUTION.

I'LL *HAPPILY* SUPERVISE, FATHER.

FOR A BRIGAND, HOWEVER, YOU'VE PROVEN YOURSELF ADMIRABLY RESOURCEFUL, AND NEW BLOOD IS ALWAYS HEALTHY FOR THE EMPIRE.

IN ADDITION TO A FULL PARDON, I OFFER YOU A COMMISSION IN THE RAVEN CORPS.

WHAT!?

I DEMAND HIS EXECUTION!

I WANT HIS HEAD!

JENA, MY LOVE.

DO NOT INTERFERE WITH MY WILL.

A COMMISSION IN THE RAVEN CORPS, EH...

AND WHAT— IF I MAY BE SO BOLD— IF I REFUSE?

I HAVE OTHER JUDGEMENTS TO MAKE THIS DAY, YOUNG DANTE.

OBSERVE THEM WHILE YOU DECIDE.

BRING FORWARD CAPTAIN ARBATOV AND HIS MEN.

HE FIGHTS WITHOUT HONOUR, TSAR VLADIMIR! HE'LL STAB YOU IN THE BACK THE FIRST CHANCE HE GETS!

HE'S A THIEF!

A THIEF WHO NONETHELESS DEFEATED A SQUAD OF HIGHLY TRAINED HUSSARS.

IMAGINE HOW THE MORALE OF MY OTHER TROOPS WOULD SUFFER IF I LET SUCH A FAILURE GO UNPUNISHED.

ARBATOV, YOU SOUGHT THE SERVICES OF A SEDUCTRESS WHILE COURTING MY DAUGHTER, JENA— AN INSULT TO IMPERIAL HONOUR!

"YOU'RE BETTER OFF WITHOUT HIM, TSARINA...

HIS MISTRESS TOLD ME ALL THE INTIMATE, INSULTING THINGS HE SAID ABOUT YOU.

HOWEVER, IN RECOGNITION OF YOUR PAST LOYALTY I WILL BE MERCIFUL.

RAVENS, FLAY THE SKINS FROM THEIR BODIES.

IF IT GROWS BACK WITHIN THE WEEK, I SHALL ACCEPT THAT AS A SIGN OF INNOCENCE AND GRANT A STAY OF EXECUTION.

NO! NO!

EEEYAAAHH!

YOUR ANSWER, YOUNG DANTE?

SO, WHEN DO I START?

AND DO I HAVE TO WEAR ONE OF THOSE DAMNED HELMETS?

NEXT PROG ▷ ALIENATION ZONE!

Nikolai Dante

PART 3

THE IMPERIAL PALACE, ST. PETERSBURG.

WASH ME.

VIGOROUSLY.

SCRIPT
Robbie Morrison

ART
Simon Fraser

LETTERS
Annie Parkhouse

AS YOU KNOW, *TSAR VLADIMIR*, ALL NEW ADMISSIONS TO THE PALACE DUNGEONS UNDERGO EXTENSIVE GENETIC SCANNING.

PRISONER NIKOLAI DANTE'S GENETIC HERITAGE AND BLOODLINE WERE UNMISTAKEABLE.

WHILE NOT A *FULL-BLOODED* MEMBER OF THE DYNASTY, THE PURITY OF HIS SYSTEM IS *MORE* THAN ENOUGH FOR YOUR PURPOSES.

I FEEL RATHER *SORRY* FOR HIM.

THE POOR BOY HAS *ABSOLUTELY* NO IDEA *WHO* OR *WHAT* HE IS.

HE'S AN ARROGANT THIEF...

I *SPARED* HIS LIFE BECAUSE OF YOUR DISCOVERY, PHYSICIAN.

IF YOU'RE MISTAKEN OR IF THE PLANS I HAVE FOR YOUNG DANTE *FAIL*...

...I WILL HAVE YOU ADMINISTERED WITH AN *ENEMA*.

A *CORROSIVE ACID* ENEMA.

ONE OF THE MOST EFFECTIVE *TORTURES* I DEVISED DURING *THE PURGES,* PYRE.

I WAS REMARKABLY IMAGINATIVE WHEN IT CAME TO DEALING WITH ENEMIES IN THE EARLY DAYS OF MY REIGN.

I THINK THE *POWER* WENT TO MY HEAD SLIGHTLY, MADE ME RATHER *DECADENT.*

DECADENT, TSAR VLADIMIR? YOU?

SURELY NOT.

MURMANSK.

THIS IS CAPTAIN DANTE OF THE IMPERIAL RAVEN CORPS.

STAND ASIDE OR FACE THE WRATH OF TSAR VLADIMIR THE CONQUEROR!

BOJEMOI!

SO MUCH FOR THE *FEARSOME* REPUTATION OF THE RAVEN CORPS!

ISN'T THE MERE SIGHT OF YOU MEANT TO HAVE THE PEASANTS FLEEING IN TERROR?

YOUR TACTICS WERE PATHETIC.

A *TRUE* RAVEN DOES NOT *DEIGN* TO SPEAK TO HIS ENEMIES.

AND A TRUE RAVEN *NEVER* SPARES THE LIVES OF THOSE WHO OPPOSE THE TSAR'S WILL.

YOU'VE A LOT TO *LEARN*, BOY.

I THINK I'VE *LEARNED* ENOUGH.

YOUR UNIFORM IS *INCOMPLETE*— YOU NEED A *HEAD* FOR YOUR BELT.

I'LL *DONATE* THIS ONE IF YOU LACK THE *STOMACH* TO CLAIM YOUR OWN.

OH, I'VE THE STOMACH ALRIGHT.

MAYBE I'LL TAKE *YOURS*.

THIS BICKERING ENDS *NOW*. REMOUNT YOUR *RAVENWINGS*, THE OBJECTIVE OF OUR MISSION IS OVER THE NEXT HILL.

THE IMPERIAL FLEET ATTACKED AN *UNIDENTIFIED* STARSHIP AFTER IT ENTERED OUR ATMOSPHERE WITHOUT PERMISSION.

WE'RE TO INVESTIGATE THE WRECK AND REPORT OUR FINDINGS TO ST. PETERSBURG.

THERE SHE IS...

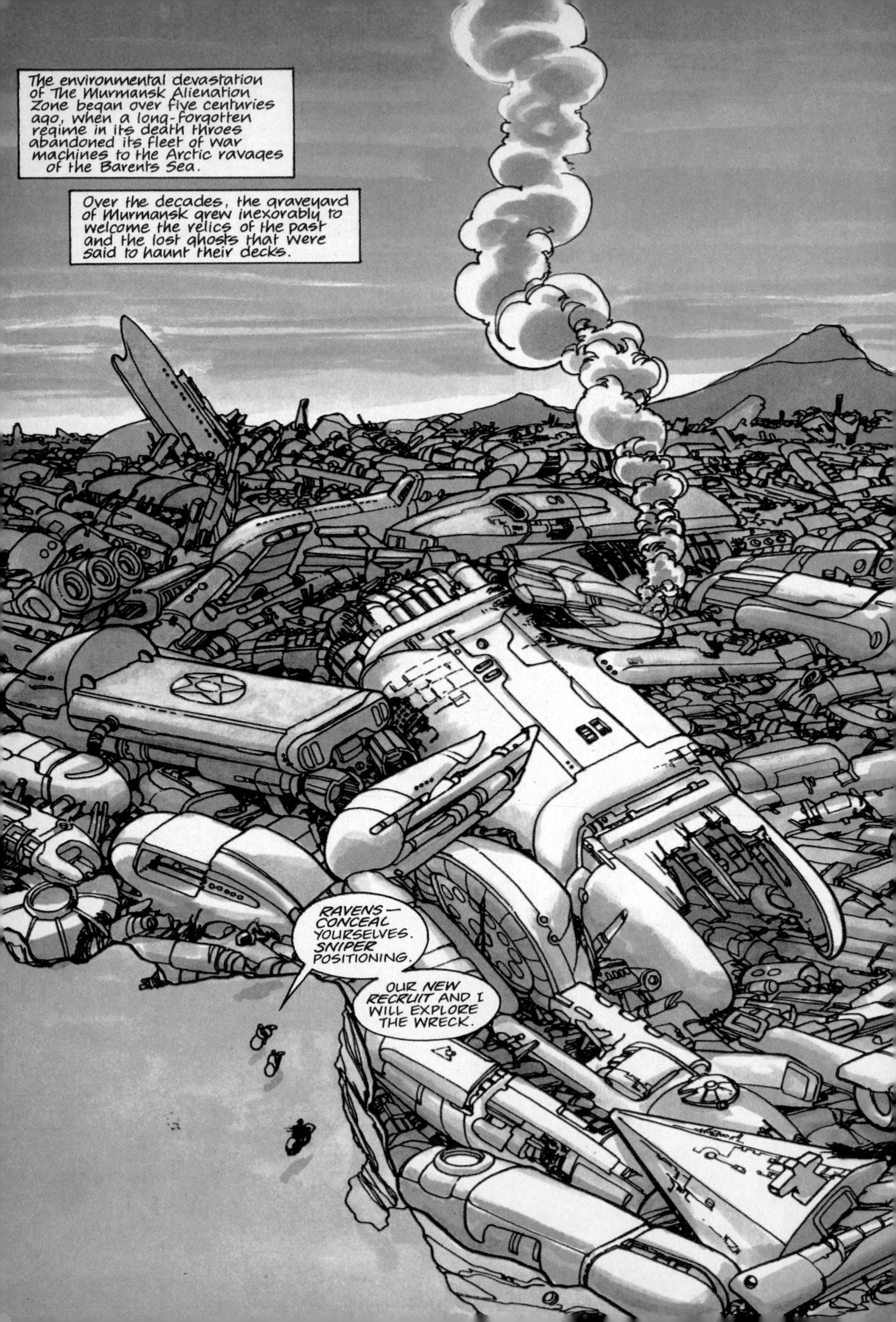
The environmental devastation of The Murmansk Alienation Zone began over five centuries ago, when a long-forgotten regime in its death throes abandoned its fleet of war machines to the Arctic ravages of the Barents Sea.
Over the decades, the graveyard of Murmansk grew inexorably to welcome the relics of the past and the lost ghosts that were said to haunt their decks.
RAVENS— CONCEAL YOURSELVES. SNIPER POSITIONING.
OUR NEW RECRUIT AND I WILL EXPLORE THE WRECK.

WHY NOT *DROP* THE COLD, ALOOF ACT, JENA?

WANT ME TO *WIGGLE* A LITTLE MORE?

YOUR 'ASS' WILL FEEL THE *THRUST* OF MY SABRE IF YOU DON'T CURB YOUR INSOLENCE!

YOU'VE BEEN WATCHING MY *ASS* SINCE WE LEFT YOUR MEN.

YOU'RE IMPORTANT TO MY FATHER FOR REASONS WHICH— BELIEVE ME, THIEF— *YOU DON'T WANT TO KNOW!*

BUT THAT IMPORTANCE WON'T BE DIMINISHED IF I *CUT* THE TONGUE FROM YOUR HEAD!

THUDD

METAPHORICALLY SPEAKING, ISN'T THAT THE SORT OF PROPOSITION I SHOULD BE TEMPTING YOU WITH?

GOOD IDEA. IT'D STOP ME ASKING AWKWARD QUESTIONS. SUCH AS...

WHY DOES AN 'UNIDENTIFIED' SHIP BEAR THE *ROMANOV CREST?* ISN'T RAIDING THE PROPERTY OF AN IMPERIAL DYNASTY AN ACT OF WAR?

SSSKKRREEK!

SSSKKRREEE!

BOJEMOI!

NEXT PROG ▷ BIRD OF PREY!

RUSSIA, 2666. ADVENTURER NIKOLAI DANTE HAS BEEN PRESSGANGED INTO JOINING THE TSAR'S RAVEN CORPS.

WHILE DANTE AND THE TSAR'S DAUGHTER, JENA, ARE INVESTIGATING A CRASHED STARSHIP IN THE MURMANSK ALIENATION ZONE, THEY ARE ATTACKED...

WHAT THE *HELL* IS THAT?!?

A *ROMANOV BIRD OF PREY!* IT'S PROGRAMMED TO PROTECT THEIR SHIP— IT WON'T STOP TILL WE'RE *DEAD!*

SSSKREEE

Nikolai Dante

PART 4

++ INTRUDERS RETREATING ++

++ ENGAGING PURSUIT MODE ++

DRAW ITS FIRE! I'LL *CLIP* ITS WINGS!

SCRIPT
ROBBIE MORRISON

ART
SIMON FRASER

LETTERS
ANNIE PARKHOUSE

YOU, *THIEF?* IT'LL *KILL* YOU!

SLKISHH

KILL ME, *JENA?*

I'M TOO COOL TO KILL!

SSSKREEEEEE

BOJEMOI!

++ MINIMAL DAMAGE SUSTAINED ++

++ TERMINATE INTRUDER ++

SSSSKREEEE

++ HALT TERMINATION ++

++ SCANNER CONFIRMS GENETIC SUITABILITY OF INTRUDER TO ACT AS HOST ++

++ INITIATE BONDING SEQUENCE BETWEEN HOST BODY AND WEAPONS CREST ++

AAAGHKKK!

CONGRATULATIONS, NIKOLAI DANTE? YOU'VE JUST BECOME THE MOST WANTED MAN IN THE EMPIRE.

AND I CAN'T THINK OF ANYONE MORE DESERVING OF THE HONOUR.

NOW, MOVE!

THE BIRD OF PREY HAS DEACTIVATED BECAUSE IT THINKS IT'S ACCOMPLISHED ITS MISSION — ITS MASTERS WON'T BE SO EASILY FOOLED.

WELL, WELL, IF IT ISN'T *THE TSAR'S* FAVOURITE DAUGHTER.

AN *ILLUSTRIOUS* VISITOR INDEED.

WHO?

PERMIT US TO INTRODUCE OURSELVES — FOR THE SAKE OF YOUR UNKEMPT COMPANION.

HONESTLY, JENA, I'D HAVE CREDITED YOU WITH *BETTER* TASTE IN MEN.

ALEKSANOR AND ALEKSANDRA ROMANOV.

HEIRS TO THE *ROMANOV* DYNASTY AND ALL ITS GLORIES. PAST, PRESENT AND *FUTURE.*

NOW THAT WE'VE DISPENSED WITH *COURT FORMALITIES*...

PLEASE EXPLAIN WHY YOU THOUGHT IT NECESSARY TO TRESPASS UPON *OUR* PROPERTY.

THE FORCES OF THE TSAR— *YOUR RULER*—MAY GO WHERE THEY PLEASE.

YOUR STARSHIP CRASHED. WE, *UH,* WERE IN THE VICINITY AND INITIATED A SEARCH FOR SURVIVORS.

HOW VERY *BENEVOLENT* OF YOU—CONSIDERING IT WAS MORE THAN LIKELY THE *TSARIST FLEET* THAT BROUGHT HER DOWN IN THE FIRST PLACE.

YET ANOTHER *DESPERATE* ATTEMPT TO GAIN POSSESSION OF THE ROMANOV POWER SOURCE.

I DON'T CARE FOR YOUR ACCUSATIONS, ROMANOV!

YOU *DARE* AIM A WEAPON AT US, MAKAROV BITCH!?

RAVENS! SNIPER FIRE!

CUT THEM DOWN!

BRRRAM

AHHHH!

BOJEMOI!

OUCH.

I HAD HOPED WE COULD BE *DIGNIFIED* ABOUT THIS, JENA, BUT THEN DIGNITY IS *NOT* A CONCEPT ONE ASSOCIATES WITH YOUR KIND.

THE TIME OF THE MAKAROV DYNASTY IS OVER.

YOUR FATHER HAS *BLED* THE EMPIRE DRY FOR TOO LONG.

IT *FESTERS* UNDER HIS TYRANNY.

TO RECLAIM ITS FORMER GLORY, IT MUST LOOK TO THE FUTURE.

WE ARE THE FUTURE.

THE *RAVEN CORPS* WISH TO ENGAGE US IN SOME FORM OF PHYSICAL ACTIVITY.

SHALL WE OBLIGE?

IT WOULD BE RUDE TO REFUSE THEM THE PLEASURE OF A DANCE. AFTER ALL, THEY RUINED OUR FAVOURITE COATS.

27

NEXT PROG ▷ DOUBLE TROUBLE!

IN THE MURMANSK ALIENATION ZONE *NIKOLAI DANTE* HAS BEEN BONDED TO A HOUSE OF ROMANOV *BIO-CREST*, MAKING HIM THE MOST WANTED MAN IN THE EMPIRE.

NOW HE IS IN THE MIDDLE OF A PITCHED BATTLE BETWEEN THE *RAVEN CORPS*, LED BY THE TSAR'S DAUGHTER JENA, AND *ROMANOV TWINS* ALEKSANDR AND ALEKSANDRA...

Nikolai Dante

PART **5**

IT MUST BE *TRUE* WHAT THEY SAY IN THE RAVEN CORPS...

THERE'S *NO GREATER HONOUR* THAN TO LAY DOWN YOUR LIFE FOR THE TSAR.

THEY CERTAINLY SEEM *MORE* THAN WILLING TO DIE TODAY...

SCRIPT
ROBBIE MORRISON
ART
SIMON FRASER
LETTERS
ANNIE PARKHOUSE

DANTE! YOU'RE AN OFFICER IN THE RAVEN CORPS! AID YOUR COMRADES!

JENA, MY COMRADES WOULD GLADLY *DANGLE* ME FROM THE GALLOWS IF THEY HAD THE CHANCE...

ANYWAY, THIS DAMNED *EAGLE'S KILLING* ME ALREADY.

I HAVEN'T FELT THIS BAD SINCE CHALLENGING *PAPA YELTSIN* TO A *VODKA-SWILLING* CONTEST...

BOJEMOI! WHAT'S HAPPENING TO MY *HANDS?!?*

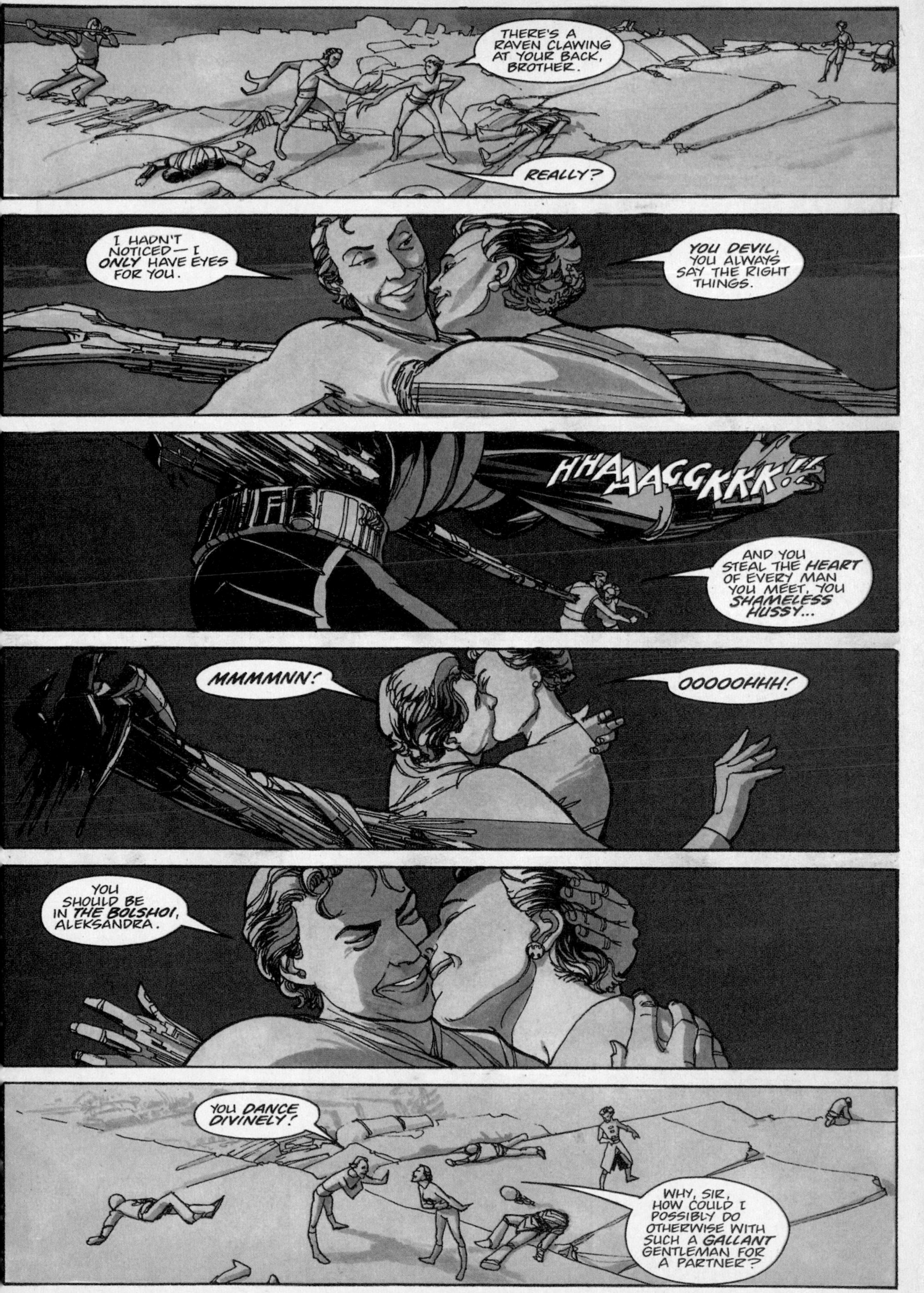

THERE'S A RAVEN CLAWING AT YOUR BACK, BROTHER.
REALLY?
I HADN'T NOTICED— I ONLY HAVE EYES FOR YOU.
YOU DEVIL, YOU ALWAYS SAY THE RIGHT THINGS.
HHAAAGGKKK!!
AND YOU STEAL THE HEART OF EVERY MAN YOU MEET, YOU SHAMELESS HUSSY...
MMMMNN!
OOOOOHHH!
YOU SHOULD BE IN THE BOLSHOI, ALEKSANDRA.
YOU DANCE DIVINELY!
WHY, SIR, HOW COULD I POSSIBLY DO OTHERWISE WITH SUCH A GALLANT GENTLEMAN FOR A PARTNER?

NOW, JENA, HOW SHOULD WE HANDLE YOUR *INDISCRETION*?

REVEAL IT TO THE EMPIRE AND CAUSE A *MAJOR* DYNASTIC SCANDAL?

OR PUNISH IT NOW WITH A *QUIET* EXECUTION?

BOTH OPTIONS ARE *VERY* TEMPTING.

YOU'D DO WELL TO FOLLOW YOUR COMPANION'S LEAD— *PROSTRATE* YOURSELF BEFORE US WHILE WE DECIDE.

IT'S *PATHETIC*, BUT ALSO *GRATIFYING*, TO SEE A MAN *BEG* IN SUCH A WAY.

IT MAKES YOU REALISE HOW *SUPERIOR* WE ROMANOVS ARE TO THE REST OF THE EMPIRE.

THERE'S *BLOOD* ON MY BOOT. LICK IT OFF, AND PERHAPS I'LL *SPARE* YOU.

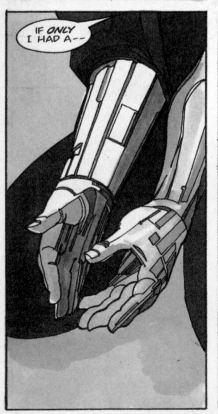

IF *ONLY* I HAD A--

A *WEAPON*?!?

COME ON, BE *QUICK* ABOUT IT.

30

GGNNYYAAHH!

I'M NOT A BEGGING MAN!

ALEKSANDRA! HE BEARS THE CREST!

IMPOSSIBLE! ONLY A *ROMANOV* BORN MAY BEAR A *WEAPONS* CREST!

AAACHKK!

COME ON, JENA!

HE CUT ME! HE CUT ME!

YOUR PAIN IS MY PAIN, BROTHER. WE'LL MAKE HIM *SUFFER!*

NANO-MINES!

YOU KNOW HOW TO SHOW A MAN A GOOD TIME, JENA. I'VE *BOOZED* MY WAY ACROSS HALF THE EMPIRE AND NEVER EVEN WOKEN UP WITH A *TATTOO*...

ONE DAY IN YOUR COMPANY AND I GET A *GARGOYLE* GRAFTED TO MY SHOULDER?

NOT TO MENTION THESE *BEAUTIES*.

WHAT THE HELL'S GOING ON?

YOU'RE AN OFFICER OF THE RAVEN CORPS. INFORMATION IS RELAYED TO YOU *ONLY* ON A *NEED-TO-KNOW* BASIS.

IS THAT A FACT? PERHAPS OUR TWIN ADMIRERS WILL BE MORE OBLIGING...

THIS WAS MEANT TO BE A *SIMPLE* EXTRACTION, ALEKSANDR. WE SHOULD CALL FOR *BACK-UP*.

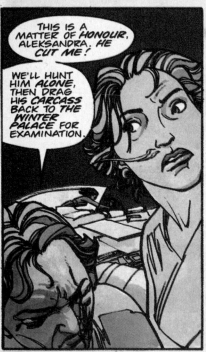

THIS IS A MATTER OF *HONOUR*, ALEKSANDRA. HE *CUT ME!*

WE'LL HUNT HIM *ALONE*, THEN DRAG HIS *CARCASS* BACK TO THE *WINTER PALACE* FOR EXAMINATION.

YOU'RE A *RECKLESS ONE*, THIEF.

WHY, TSARINA JENA— *FLATTERY*'LL GET YOU *EVERYWHERE*...

THE ROMANOV DYNASTY HAVE DEVELOPED THE MOST POWERFUL *BIO-WEAPON* IN THE EMPIRE, FASHIONED IN THE FORM OF THEIR ANCIENT *COAT-OF-ARMS*.

THE *WEAPONS CREST* POSES A GREAT THREAT TO THE TSAR'S REIGN. HE MUST LEARN ITS SECRETS AND DEVELOP SIMILAR TECHNOLOGY FOR HIS OWN FORCES.

'THE WEAPONS CREST SYMBIOTICALLY *BONDS* ONLY WITH THE *ROMANOV ELITE*. THEIR GENETIC PURITY HAS BEEN ENHANCED BY A BREEDING PROGRAMME INITIATED BY *DIMITRI ROMANOV, DYNASTY PATRIARCH,* TO STRENGTHEN THEIR FALSE CLAIM TO THE EMPIRE.

'*BEARING THE CREST* GIVES THE ROMANOVS COMBAT CAPABILITIES UNIQUELY ATTUNED TO THEIR INDIVIDUAL PHYSICAL AND PSYCHOLOGICAL PROFILES.

'IT MANIFESTS ITSELF AS *NANOTECHNOLOGY* IN THE TWINS, FILLING THEIR SYSTEMS WITH *MICROSCOPIC DROIDS* WHICH CAN HEAL ALMOST ANY WOUND, FORM *BIO-BLADES* OR BE LAUNCHED FROM THE BODY AS INVISIBLE EXPLOSIVES.

'THE CRESTS ARE PRODUCED BY *UNKNOWN TECHNOLOGY* AT A SECRET OFFWORLD LOCATION. WE INTERCEPTED THE TRANSPORTATION OF THE LATEST ONE — *WITH YOU!'*

AND WHY'S THE DAMNED THING SO ATTRACTED TO ME?

ISN'T IT OBVIOUS FROM YOUR COMPLETE LACK OF *HONOUR* AND *INTEGRITY?*

YOU'RE BORN OF THE CRUELLEST KILLERS IN THE THIEVES' WORLD...

YOU'RE ONE OF *THEM.*

YOU'RE A *ROMANOV!*

33

NEXT PROG ▷ SIBLING RIVALRY!
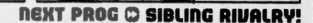

IN THE MURMANSK ALIENATION ZONE NIKOLAI DANTE HAS BEEN BONDED WITH A ROMANOV BIO-CREST, MAKING HIM THE MOST WANTED MAN IN THE EMPIRE.

NOW DANTE HAS LEARNED FROM THE TSAR'S DAUGHTER JENA THAT HE IS OF ARISTOCRATIC BLOOD...

A GENESCAN CONFIRMED YOUR HERITAGE WHILE YOU WERE IN IMPERIAL CUSTODY. NO DOUBT ABOUT IT, YOU'RE A ROMANOV, ALRIGHT.

BASTARD SON OF A NOBLE HOUSE, EH...

Nikolai Dante

SCRIPT
ROBBIE MORRISON

ART
SIMON FRASER

COLOURS
ALISON KIRKPATRICK

LETTERS
ANNIE PARKHOUSE

PART 6

YOU DIDN'T KNOW YOUR PARENTS?

ONLY MAMA— KATARINA DANTE.

SHE WASN'T VERY SPECIFIC ABOUT MY FATHER'S IDENTITY...

KATARINA DANTE!? THE PIRATE-QUEEN!?

SHE ABANDONED ME WHEN I WAS 11 OR 12, I'M NOT SURE WHICH...

SHE INSISTS ON ROBBING THE EMPIRE BLIND WITH AN ALL-FEMALE CREW.

THEY DIDN'T HAVE MUCH IN THE WAY OF MALE FACILITIES, AND I WAS AN EARLY DEVELOPER.

WELL, JENA, YOU'VE GOT YOUR PRECIOUS WEAPONS CREST— AND ME INTO THE BARGAIN. NOW WHAT?

WE EVADE THE ROMANOVS AND RETURN TO ST. PETERSBURG.

WHERE I'LL BE SLICED AND DICED BY THE TSAR'S SCIENTISTS AS THEY TRY TO UNLOCK THE SECRETS OF THE CREST AND ADAPT IT FOR IMPERIAL USE.

YOU'LL BE HANDSOMELY REWARDED, THIEF.

IF YOU SURVIVE.

USURPER OF THE ROMANOV CREST!

YOU CANNOT ESCAPE!

OUR CRESTS CAN TRACK YOURS WITHOUT FAIL!

THE HULL OF YOUR CRAFT IS *BREACHED* IN SEVERAL PLACES! IT CANNOT REMAIN AFLOAT FOR LONG!

YOU HAVE THREE CHOICES! *SURRENDER* AND WE MAY BE MERCIFUL! FACE US IN *COMBAT* AND *DIE!*

OR *DROWN* AND WE'LL *TRAWL* FOR YOUR CORPSE LATER!

DECIDE!

YOU WANT ME, YOU NOBLE SCUM!? COME AND GET ME!

JENA, MAKE YOUR WAY DOWN THE CORRIDOR, USE ONE OF THEIR BREACHES TO ESCAPE. I'LL KEEP THEM BUSY.

WHAT!?

YOU HEARD THEM, *I* CAN'T ESCAPE — BUT *YOU* CAN. YOU'RE THE *FUTURE EMPRESS* OF OUR WORLD. YOU *HAVE* TO LIVE!

I'M JUST A *THIEF.* LIVE OR DIE, I'M *NOTHING.*

BUT IN THE BRIEF TIME WE'VE HAD TOGETHER, JENA MAKAROV, I'VE KNOWN *HONOUR* AND *NOBILITY*... MAYBE EVEN *LOVE.*

NIKOLAI...

THINK OF ME, MILADY?

SOMETIMES?

THE THINGS I SAY TO GET INTO PEOPLE'S PANTS!

WHOA! HOLD YOUR FIRE! I'M WITH YOU!

I'M ONE OF YOU!

OUR PREY'S CHANGED HIS TUNE. *NOBLE SCUM?* WASN'T THAT WHAT HE CALLED US?

I SAID THAT TO SEND THE TSARINA ON HER WAY.

PRECIPITATING A CONFLICT WITH THE TSAR IS THE LAST THING WE ROMANOVS NEED. *NO?*

WE ROMANOVS?

OF COURSE!

I'VE NO IDEA WHO DID THE *DIRTY DEED*, BUT MY FATHER IS A ROMANOV. HOW ELSE COULD THE CREST HAVE BONDED WITH ME?

I'M READY TO TAKE MY RIGHTFUL PLACE IN THE ROMANOV DYNASTY AND ACCEPT THE RESPONSIBILITIES OF MY HERITAGE...

AND, I *SUPPOSE*, WHATEVER *WEALTH* THAT ENTAILS...

DID YOU HEAR THAT ALEKSANDR? A *NEW ADDITION* TO THE FAMILY!

WHAT *THRILLING* TIMES WE COULD HAVE TOGETHER! WHAT *FUN*...

IF HE WASN'T A *SEWER-BRED BASTARD!!*

WOOOAAARGH!

PRECEDENCE IS *EVERYTHING* TO AN IMPERIAL DYNASTY.

WE ROMANOVS HAVE STRIVED AFTER *GENETIC PURITY* FOR GENERATIONS...

YOU THINK WE'D LET A *HALF-BLOOD* LIKE YOU JOIN US!?

I DON'T THINK WE SHOULD EVEN *TAINT* OUR BIO-BLADES WITH YOUR *BASTARD* BLOOD...

JUST IN CASE WE *CATCH* SOMETHING...

NANO-MINES, BROTHER?

NANO-MINES, SISTER?

TELL ME, I'VE BEEN AN ONLY CHILD FOR 20-ODD YEARS...

IS THIS WHAT THEY MEAN BY *SIBLING RIVALRY?*

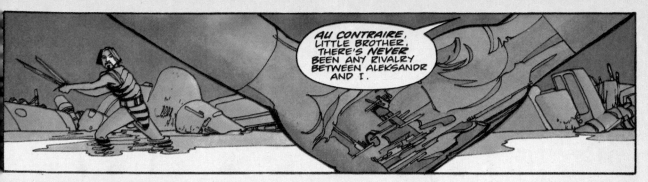

AU CONTRAIRE, LITTLE BROTHER, THERE'S *NEVER* BEEN ANY RIVALRY BETWEEN ALEKSANDR AND I.

SINCE BIRTH, WE'VE *LIVED* AS ONE, *LOVED* AS ONE...

THOUGHT AS ONE...

AND *TALKED* AS ONE...

BUT OUR MOST CHERISHED DREAM ONLY BECAME REALITY WHEN FATHER BLESSED US WITH OUR WEAPONS CRESTS...

AND ALLOWED US TO *BECOME* ONE!

BOJEMOI!

IN THE MURMANSK ALIENATION ZONE NIKOLAI DANTE HAS BEEN BONDED WITH A ROMANOV BIO-CREST, MAKING HIM THE MOST 'WANTED MAN IN THE EMPIRE.

NOW DANTE FIGHTS ROMANOV TWINS ALEKSANDR AND ALEKSANDRA, WHO HAVE MERGED WITH EACH OTHER...

IMPRESSIVE SIGHT, AREN'T WE? BOTH MALE AND FEMALE.

THE PERFECT BEING!

Nikolai Dante

PART 7

YOU SHOULD BE HONOURED TO HAVE US AS YOUR EXECUTIONER!

SCRIPT
ROBBIE MORRISON

ART
SIMON FRASER

COLOURS
ALISON KIRKPATRICK

LETTERS
ANNIE PARKHOUSE

THE PLEASURE'S ALL YOURS—

—SO'S THE PAIN!

40

WHICH PART OF THE *PERFECT BEING* DID THAT HURT MOST?

MALE OR FEMALE?

YOU'LL NEVER BE A TRUE ROMANOV!

BOJEMOI!!

A *LOWBORN BASTARD*— THAT'S *ALL YOU ARE*, ALL YOU'LL *EVER BE!*

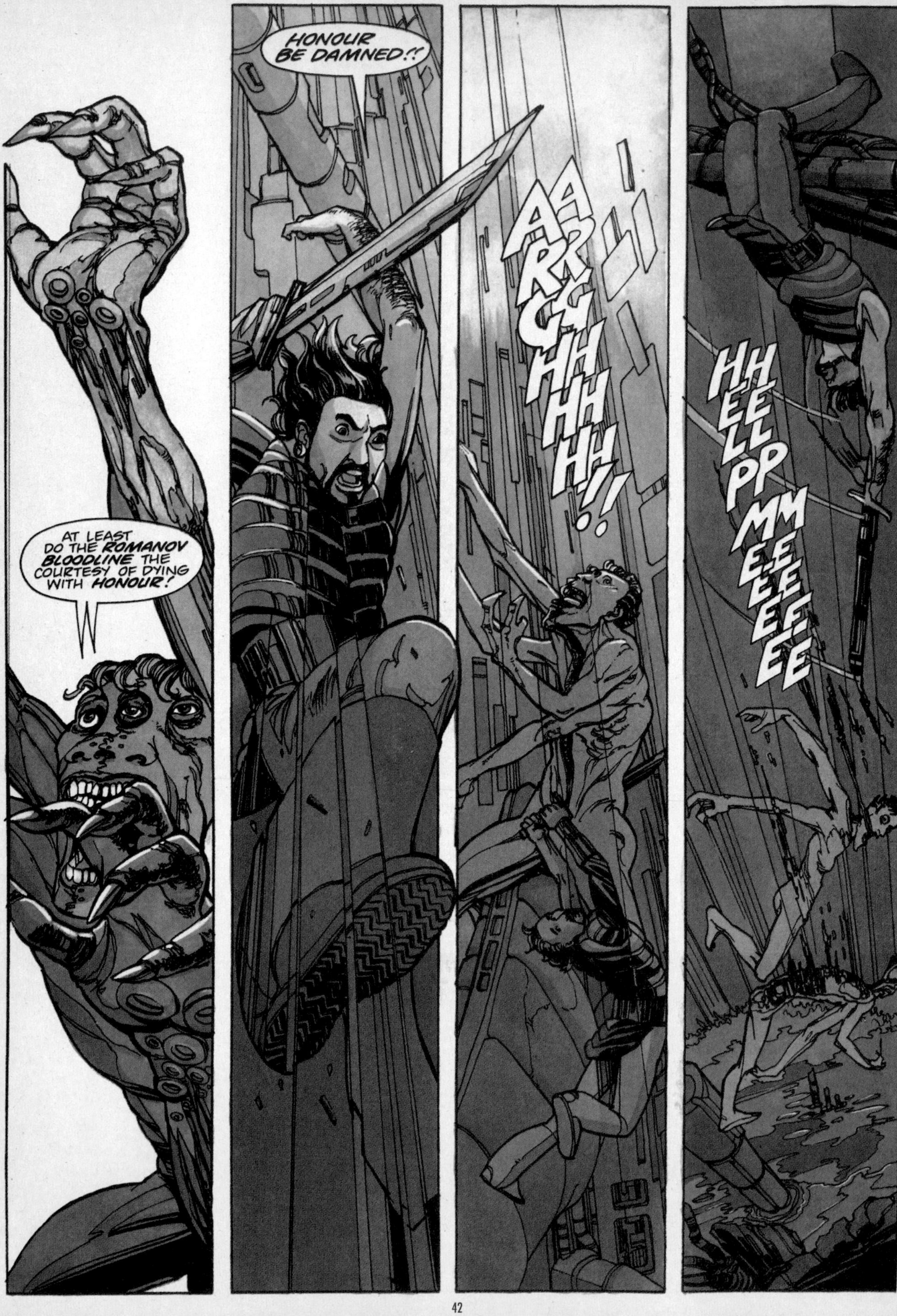
AT LEAST DO THE ROMANOV BLOODLINE THE COURTESY OF DYING WITH HONOUR!
HONOUR BE DAMNED!!
AARRGHHHHH!!
HHEELLPP MMEEEEEE

IF I'D HAD THE ARISTOCRATIC UPBRINGING YOU THINK ME SO *UNWORTHY* OF, I MIGHT ENGAGE IN ACTS OF SELFLESS NOBILITY...

...BUT I *DOUBT* IT!

YOU *HAVE* PROVED YOURSELF WORTHY. YOU *ARE* ONE OF US

YOU ARE A *ROMANOV!*

THE NAME'S *DANTE. NIKOLAI DANTE.*

THE *WORLD* IS GOING TO BE HEARING A *LOT* OF IT.

IT'S THE *LAST THING* YOU'LL EVER *HEAR!*

YOU HAVE A DISTINCT TALENT FOR *SURVIVAL*, NIKOLAI DANTE.

LIKE I SAID, JENA... I'M JUST *TOO COOL* TO KILL.

I'M BEGINNING TO THINK YOUR *NOBLE* SACRIFICE OF EARLIER WAS SOMEWHAT *LESS-THAN-SINCERE.*

WOMEN ARE *ALWAYS* SUSPICIOUS OF ME...

WITH GOOD REASON.

YOUR COMMISSION IN THE RAVEN CORPS IS HEREBY *REVOKED.* CONSIDER YOURSELF *MY PRISONER.*

I LIKE BEING MY OWN MAN. YOU WANT MY *FREEDOM*, YOU'LL HAVE TO *TAME* ME FIRST.

THINK YOU'RE *WOMAN* ENOUGH?

I WAS TRAINED IN THE ARTS OF WAR BY THE *FINEST* MILITARY COMMANDERS IN THE EMPIRE.

AND I LEARNED TO FIGHT IN THE *SLEAZIEST* BARS OF THE THIEVES' WORLD.

LET'S GET IT ON?

EN GARDE, THIEF!

Y'KNOW, JENA? THERE ARE *BETTER* WAYS TO TAME A MAN...

WHY DON'T WE SLIP OUT OF THESE WET CLOTHES AND I'LL SHOW YOU A FEW?

44

THE ONLY TIME I WANT TO SEE YOU *NAKED* IS WHEN YOU'RE STRAPPED TO THE RACK HAVING YOUR *GENITALS* CUT OFF AND DANGLED IN FRONT OF YOU!

NOW, LOSE THE BLADES OR I'LL *SLICE* THAT STUPID GRIN FROM *EAR* TO *EAR!*

WHOA! OKAY, OKAY! YOU HAVE MY WORD, I *SURRENDER!*

A LITTLE *HUMILITY,* THAT'S MORE LIKE IT.

AM I *WOMAN* ENOUGH, NOW?

NEVER TRUST THE WORD OF A *THIEF,* MILADY!

AS FOR BEING *WOMAN* ENOUGH, THERE'S ONLY *ONE* WAY WE'LL FIND THAT OUT...

NEXT PROG ▷ THE ROMANOV DYNASTY!

Dante

THE ROMANOV DYNASTY

Script: Robbie Morrison

Art: Simon Fraser

Colors: Alison Kirkpatrick

Letters: Ellie de Ville, Annie Parkhouse

Originally published in *2000 AD* Progs 1042-1049

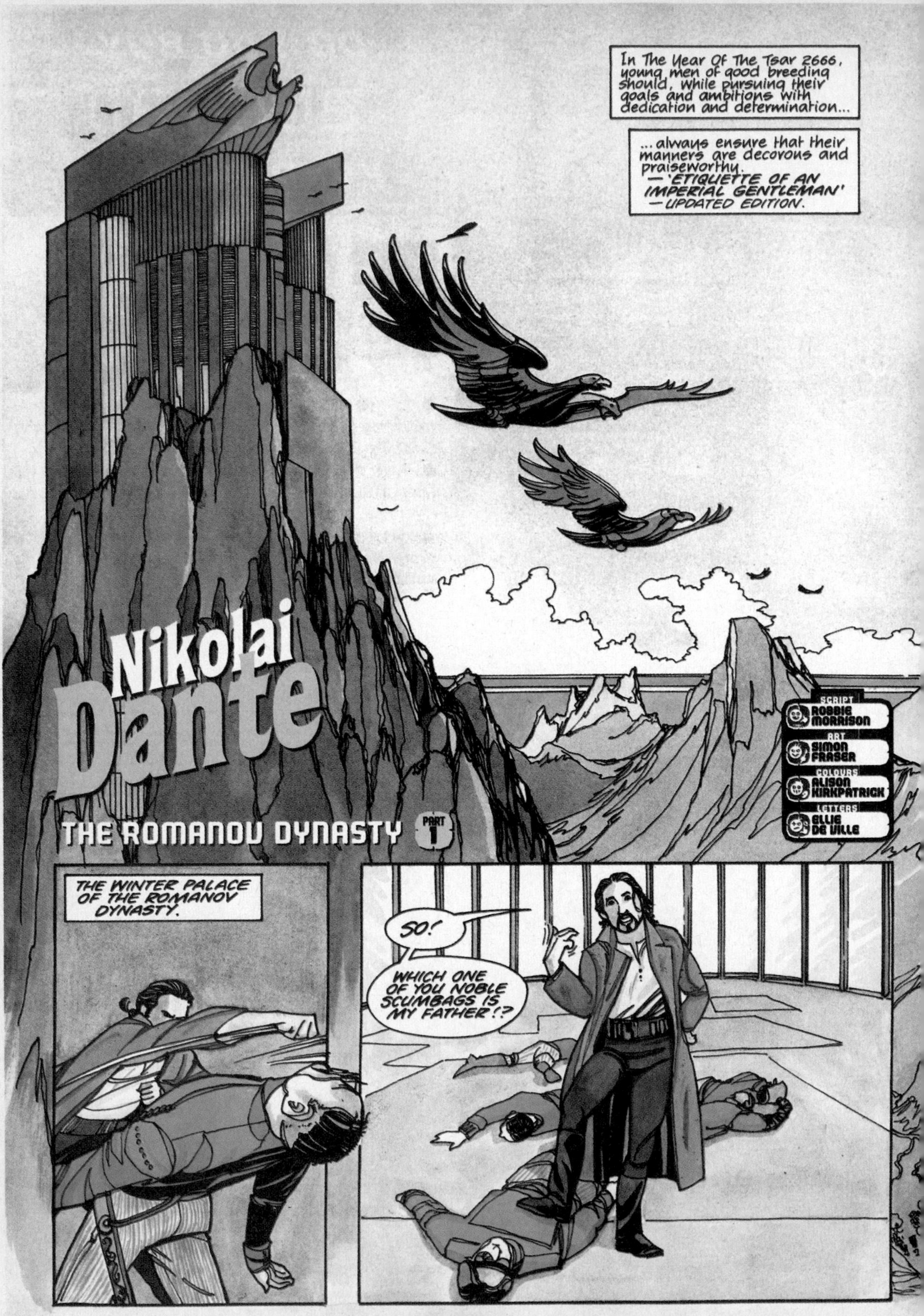

In The Year Of The Tsar 2666, young men of good breeding should, while pursuing their goals and ambitions with dedication and determination...
...always ensure that their manners are decorous and praiseworthy.
—'ETIQUETTE OF AN IMPERIAL GENTLEMAN'
—UPDATED EDITION.
Nikolai Dante
THE ROMANOV DYNASTY PART 1
SCRIPT ROBBIE MORRISON
ART SIMON FRASER
COLOURS ALISON KIRKPATRICK
LETTERS ELLIE DE VILLE
THE WINTER PALACE OF THE ROMANOV DYNASTY.
SO!
WHICH ONE OF YOU NOBLE SCUMBAGS IS MY FATHER!?

FOR YOUR SAKE, *BOY*...

I HOPE THERE'S MORE TO YOUR CLAIM THAN SIMPLE *INSANITY* OR DELUSIONS OF GRANDEUR.

THE NAME'S *DANTE. NIKOLAI DANTE.*

AND THERE'S A LOT MORE TO ME THAN MEETS THE EYE— ONLY A *ROMANOV BORN* CAN BEAR THE CREST!

AND WHAT DO YOU EXPECT TO CLAIM AS YOUR *BIRTHRIGHT*?

NOTHING *TOO* OSTENTATIOUS, *LORD DMITRI.*

POWER, RANK, WEALTH, USE OF THE ROMANOV HAREM, OR A *PRIVATE* ONE OF MY OWN.

MAYBE A *TITLE—COUNT DANTE'S* GOT A CERTAIN RING TO IT.

BEARING THE CREST AND BEING *WORTHY* OF IT ARE ENTIRELY DIFFERENT THINGS, BOY.

I DISPATCHED TWO OF MY FAMILY TO RECOVER THAT CREST. SHOULD I ASSUME YOU HAVE SINCE DISPATCHED THEM FROM THIS WORLD?

I ESCAPED THE TSAR'S FORCES IMMEDIATELY AFTER THEY FORCED ME TO BOND WITH THE CREST. I ENCOUNTERED *NO* ROMANOVS UNTIL ARRIVING HERE.

AND IT *TEARS* AT MY HEART TO THINK THAT I MAY HAVE *LOST* BROTHERS OR SISTERS WITHOUT *EVER* MEETING THEM...

ALMOST AS MUCH AS IT TURNS MY STOMACH TO HEAR YOUR LIES, THIEF!

JENA MAKAROV, THE TSAR'S DAUGHTER. WE CAUGHT HER SCALING THE NORTH FACE. SENT THREE MEN TO THEIR DEATHS BEFORE WE OVERPOWERED HER.

THIS MAN, NIKOLAI DANTE, IS A FUGITIVE FROM IMPERIAL JUSTICE!

THE TREACHEROUS SWINE DECEIVED ME IN MURMANSK— I'VE PURSUED HIM OVER HALF THE EMPIRE.

HAND HIM OVER IN THE NAME OF THE TSAR!

DON'T ADDRESS US AS IF WE WERE YOUR SUBJECTS, GIRL.

THE ROMANOV DYNASTY HAS A FAR GREATER CLAIM TO THE THRONE THAN YOUR OWN.

YOU SHOULDN'T BE SO ARROGANT, LORD DMITRI. NOT WHEN TWO OF YOUR CHILDREN ARE MISSING.

PERHAPS YOUR WEAPONS CRESTS AREN'T AS INVINCIBLE AS YOU THINK.

Are you trying to get us both killed!?

The only thing I'm devoting my life to seeing killed is you, Dante!

DON'T LISTEN TO HER, LORD DMITRI!

SHE SUFFERS FROM WINDSOR SYNDROME. POWER AND WEALTH HAVE DRIVEN HER MAD— SHE CHASES ME AROUND LIKE A LUST-CRAZED SEDUCTRESS.

WHERE ARE *ALEKSANDR* AND *ALEKSANDRA?*

AT THE *BOTTOM* OF THE *BARENTS SEA.*

THEY LAUNCHED AN UNPROVOKED ATTACK ON THE *RAVEN CORPS,* AND PAID THE PRICE *ALL* THE TSAR'S ENEMIES PAY.

I WOULDN'T BE A GOOD FATHER IF I DIDN'T SEEK *RETRIBUTION.*

LET THE RECORDS SHOW THAT JENA MAKAROV RECEIVED THE *FAIREST* OF TRIALS.

PROVE YOUR *LOYALTY* TO US, YOUNG DANTE!

EXECUTE THE MAKAROV BITCH. *SLOWLY* AND *PAINFULLY.*

Jena...

FATHER! SOMETHING'S APPROACHING THE WINTER PALACE—*FAR* BIGGER THAN ANY KNOWN IMPERIAL BATTLECRAFT!

OPEN THE OBSERVATION BAY.

BOJEMOI!

DID YOU REALLY THINK I'D ENTER THIS *EAGLES'* NEST WITHOUT A FEW *MINOR* PRECAUTIONS?

THE IMPERIAL PALACE!

BY ORDER OF *TSAR VLADIMIR THE CONQUEROR*, THE *HOUSE OF ROMANOV* STANDS ACCUSED OF THE FOLLOWING OFFENCES:

AND THE HARBOURING OF FUGITIVE *NIKOLAI DANTE*, A COMMON THIEF UNDER SENTENCE OF *DEATH*.

ESPIONAGE ACTIVITY INTENDED TO UNDERMINE TSARIST RULE AND IMPERIAL LAW; INDEFENSIBLE ASSAULTS ON THE RAVEN CORPS IN THE REGION OF MURMANSK...

OF COURSE YOU REALISE...

THIS MEANS *WAR*.

EXT PROG ⟫ 'COME AND HAVE A GO IF YOU THINK YOU'RE HARD ENOUGH...'

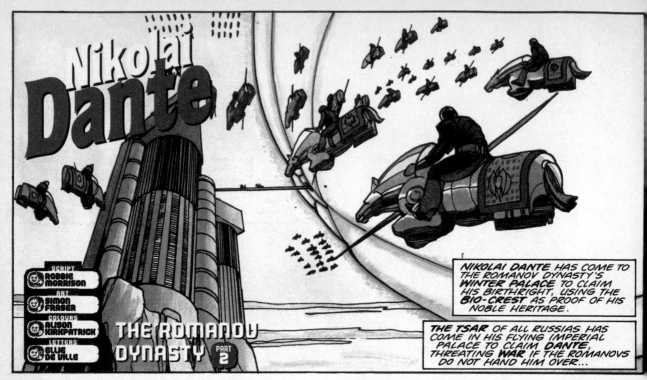

Nikolai Dante

SCRIPT
ROBBIE MORRISON

ART
SIMON FRASER

COLOURS
ALISON KIRKPATRICK

LETTERS
ELLIE DE VILLE

THE ROMANOV DYNASTY PART 2

NIKOLAI DANTE HAS COME TO THE ROMANOV DYNASTY'S *WINTER PALACE* TO CLAIM HIS BIRTHRIGHT, USING THE *BIO-CREST* AS PROOF OF HIS NOBLE HERITAGE.

THE *TSAR* OF ALL RUSSIAS HAS COME IN HIS FLYING IMPERIAL PALACE TO CLAIM *DANTE*, THREATENING *WAR* IF THE ROMANOVS DO NOT HAND HIM OVER...

THIS *POOR BOY* HAS BEEN SENTENCED TO DEATH BY MY COURT, ROMANOV!

SURRENDER HIM TO ME, AND I WILL VIEW YOUR OTHER OFFENCES WITH LENIENCY.

I THINK NOT— BUT PERHAPS I SPEAK OUT OF TURN?

YOUNG DANTE IS *NOTHING* IF NOT HIS OWN MAN. HE MAKES HIS OWN CHOICES IN THIS WORLD...

YOUR CONCERN FOR MY WELFARE IS *TOUCHING*, TSAR VLADIMIR, BUT BLOOD *IS* THICKER THAN WATER.

HOW CAN I DESERT MY FAMILY WHEN I'VE JUST FOUND THEM?

SPOKEN LIKE A TRUE ROMANOV!

BLOOD IS INDEED THICKER THAN WATER, BUT IT SATISFIES THE *THIRST* MORE.

I LOOK FORWARD TO SAMPLING *YOURS*, BOY.

THERE'S LITTLE POINT IN CONTINUING THIS DISCUSSION AT THE MOMENT. WE WILL RECONVENE WITH OUR *COUNCILS OF WAR* IN ATTENDANCE. THREE HOURS?

AGREED.

BEFORE WE PART, THERE IS A SMALL MATTER OF *PERSONAL HONOUR* TO BE SETTLED.

CAPTAIN?

DANTE, YOU THIEVING DOG!

I AM *CAPTAIN ARBATOV* OF THE TSAR'S OWN CUIRASSEIRS!

MY BROTHER WAS *SKINNED ALIVE* BECAUSE OF YOU!

I DEMAND SATISFACTION THROUGH TRIAL BY COMBAT!

HE WAS CHALLENGING YOU TO A *DUEL*.

WELL, HE *LOST*.

A *FORMAL* DUEL. ARRANGED TIMES, CHOICE OF WEAPONS.

THE ROMANOVS ARE THE *OLDEST* IMPERIAL DYNASTY, STRONG UPHOLDERS OF FORMALITY AND TRADITION.

YOU'RE MEANT TO BECOME PART OF *THAT*?

GIVE YOU ENOUGH *ROPE*, THIEF, YOU'RE SURE TO *HANG* YOURSELF.

DANTE'S *IMPUDENCE* CANNOT GO UNPUNISHED— WE'LL FIND SOME OTHER WAY OF *DEFUSING* THE ROMANOV CREST.

WHO AMONGST THE *SCARLET WRAITHS* IS BEST QUALIFIED TO ASSASSINATE HIM?

I *AM*, TSAR VLADIMIR.

IF APPREHENDED, THE ASSASSIN MUST BE SEEN TO BE ACTING ON THEIR OWN.

YOU'RE MY *LORD PROTECTOR, PYRE*. I CAN'T RISK LOSING YOU.

THEN *MARALIS*.

UUHHH...

YOUR *CONSORT*?

SHE'S AS LOYAL TO YOU AS I AM, SIRE.

YOUR *HONOUR* AND DEDICATION TO DUTY ARE ADMIRABLE, PYRE...

AS WAS THAT OF THE *ARBATOVS*. THEIR FAMILY WAS ONCE A *MOST* EFFICIENT PART OF THE MILITARY MACHINE.

HOW THE MIGHTY HAVE FALLEN...

THE ROMANOV WEAPONS RESEARCH FACILITY.

BEARING THE *WEAPONS CREST* AND THE *CYBORGANIC TECHNOLOGY* WITHIN IT GIVES THE ROMANOV ELITE COMBAT CAPABILITIES UNIQUELY ATTUNED TO THEIR INDIVIDUAL CHARACTERS.

BUT YOU'RE A *HALF-BREED*, LITTLE BROTHER. DON'T EXPECT TOO MUCH.

PERHAPS IT'S DUE TO YOUR *SHALLOW* NATURE, BUT YOUR CREST MANIFESTS ITSELF AS LITTLE MORE THAN *BIO-BLADES*, HEIGHTENED SENSES, A *MINOR* PHYSICAL HEALING FACTOR AND A *SYMBIOTIC BATTLE COMPUTER* THAT RESPONDS ONLY TO YOU.

In addition to combat duties, I am bound to educate you in the ways of the aristocracy and mould you into a potential ruler of the Empire.

Not an easy task.

IT *HASN'T* BEEN VERY RESPONSIVE SO FAR...

Your words carry such *little* substance that they deserve *no* response.

DIAVOLO!

IT'S IN MY HEAD!

Please maintain a *semblance* of dignity.

57

CAN'T YOU JUST ACCESS DYNASTY RECORDS TO FIND OUT WHICH OF THE *RANDY* ROMANOVS SIRED ME?

There are strange gaps in my databanks—no doubt due to having bonded with your inferior genes.

The family histories of the appropriate period should record encounters between your mother and the Romanovs. They may yield some clue to your father's identity.

Don't move your lips when you read. People will think you've an uneducated barbarian.

I *AM*.

AND *PROUD* OF IT.

FROM WHAT I WAS TOLD, I SAW YOU MORE AS A MAN OF *ACTION* THAN A MAN OF *WORDS*, NIKOLAI DANTE.

APPEARANCES CAN BE DECEIVING.

YOU DON'T LOOK LIKE ANY LIBRARIAN I'VE EVER SEEN BEFORE.

LIBRARIAN?

THE TSAR'S IS NOT THE ONLY DYNASTY THAT EMPLOYS *SEDUCTRESSES*. WE'VE BEEN TOLD TO EXTEND *EVERY* POSSIBLE HOSPITALITY TO YOU.

Dante. Things are *not* as they seem...

ADVISE ME *ALL* YOU WANT IN OTHER MATTERS, CREST, BUT IF THERE'S ONE THING I KNOW, IT'S *WOMEN*.

THE VOICE OF *EXPERIENCE*...

THERE'S AN OLD SAYING—'COME AND HAVE A GO IF YOU THINK YOU'RE *HARD ENOUGH*.'

SOME OF THOSE BOOKS ARE *PRICELESS* ANTIQUES.

I'M A *NEW MAN!* I DON'T RESPECT *ANYTHING* OLDER THAN ME!

If there's one thing you know, it's women...

You are currently locked in a rather less-than-erotic embrace with an *Abraxian Shapeshifter* in the service of the Tsar.

It is, however, the *female* of the species...

BOJEMOI!

NEXT PROG ◗ THE ART OF DIPLOMACY!

NIKOLAI DANTE IS NOW A MEMBER OF THE ROMANOV DYNASTY, THANKS TO THE SENTIENT *WEAPONS BIO-CREST* BONDED TO HIS BODY.

BUT DANTE'S PRESENCE AT THE ROMANOV *WINTER PALACE* THREATENS TO CAUSE WAR WITH THE TSAR, WHO'S FLYING *IMPERIAL PALACE* IS NEARBY.

DANTE'S SEARCH TO FIND WHICH ROMANOV IS HIS *FATHER* TOOK HIM TO THE DYNASTY'S *LIBRARY*, WHERE A *BEAUTIFUL WOMAN* CATCHES HIS EYE.

Nikolai Dante

UNFORTUNATELY, SHE IS ACTUALLY A *SHAPE-SHIFTING ALIEN* SENT BY THE TSAR TO *ASSASSINATE* DANTE.

THE ROMANOV DYNASTY PART 3

SCRIPT
ROBBIE MORRISON

ART
SIMON FRASER

COLOURS
ALISON KIRKPATRICK

LETTERS
ANNIE PARKHOUSE

HHHLLGH!

YOU SHOULD BE WARY OF *WHO* AND *WHAT* YOU *KISS*, THIEF!

AAAANK

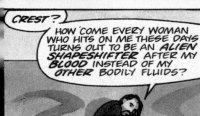

CREST?

HOW COME EVERY WOMAN WHO HITS ON ME THESE DAYS TURNS OUT TO BE AN *ALIEN SHAPESHIFTER* AFTER MY *BLOOD* INSTEAD OF MY *OTHER* BODILY FLUIDS?

Perhaps you've overestimated your appeal to the opposite sex.

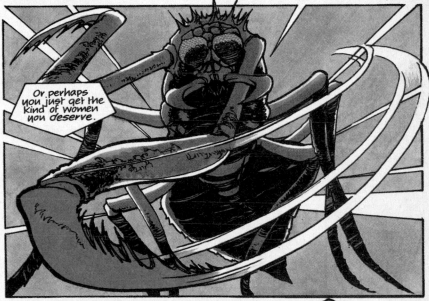

Or, perhaps you just get the kind of women you deserve.

Y'KNOW, CREST, SOMETHING TELLS ME THIS *ISN'T* THE BEGINNING OF A BEAUTIFUL FRIENDSHIP.

HHAAAA!!!

HUH?

HMPH!

SURRENDER, THIEF!

YOU HAVEN'T A CHANCE.

THE GREATEST PREDATORS IN ALL THE EMPIRE ARE MINE TO BECOME!!

THE IMPERIAL PALACE AND THE WINTER PALACE.

THIS IS BECOMING *FARCICAL*, DMITRI...

THAT TWO GREAT HOUSES SUCH AS OURS CAN BE TREATED SO *IGNOBLY*. HERE WE ARE ON THE BRINK OF *WAR*—

A WAR OF *YOUR* INSTIGATION, VLADIMIR.

—AND THE MAIN OBJECT OF OUR DISPUTE HASN'T EVEN *DEIGNED* TO SHOW HIS FACE.

WHERE IS *NIKOLAI DANTE?*

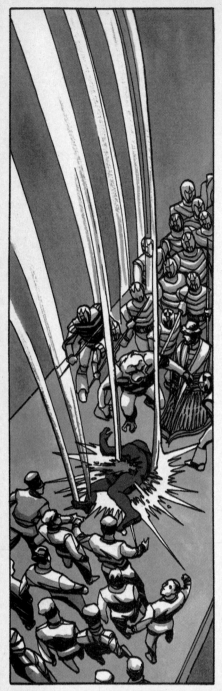

NOT TOO LATE TO DROP IN, IS IT?

I'VE BEEN THE VICTIM OF A VICIOUS ASSASSINATION ATTEMPT BY THE TSAR'S OWN *SCARLET WRAITHS!*

AND AS IF NEARLY LOSING MY LIFE WASN'T ENOUGH...

I HAD TO *KISS* THAT MONSTROSITY AS WELL!

NOT EVEN THE *SICKEST PERVERT* IN THE EMPIRE SHOULD HAVE TO ENDURE *THAT!*

MARALIS'S ACT WAS *NOT* CARRIED OUT BY IMPERIAL DECREE. SHE MUST HAVE TAKEN IT UPON HERSELF TO AVENGE DANTE'S INSULTS TO MY HONOUR.

JUST AS *ALEKSANDR* AND *ALEKSANDRA'S* ATTACK UPON YOUR FORCES DID *NOT* RECEIVE *MY* OFFICIAL SANCTION.

PERHAPS, THEN, *BOTH* OUR HOUSES ARE GUILTY OF MISCONDUCT— ALBEIT BY *DEFAULT.*

MEN LIKE *YOU* AND *I* INSPIRE SUCH LOYALTY IN OUR SUBJECTS THAT *MISGUIDED* ACTS OF *DEVOTION* ARE BOUND TO OCCUR OUTSIDE OUR CONTROL.

DETENTE, DMITRI?

AND I SHALL COMMUTE YOUNG DANTE'S DEATH SENTENCE. YOU MAY HAVE THE PLEASURE OF HIS COMPANY.

DETENTE, VLADIMIR.

AND I SHALL *NOT* PURSUE YOUR DAUGHTER JENA OVER THE DEATHS OF MY CHILDREN.

IN ALL THE THIEVES' WORLD THERE'S *NO* GREATER LIARS THAN THE NOBLE HOUSES THEMSELVES...

IT'S CALLED *DIPLOMACY,* DANTE.

PROBABLY A CONCEPT BEYOND YOUR UNDERSTANDING.

MARALIS WAS MY *CONSORT,* THIEF!

A PART OF HER LIVES ON WITHIN ME.

ONE DAY, *THAT* PART WILL CLAIM *YOUR* LIFE...

DIPLOMACY...

I'LL HAVE TO *LEARN* THAT SOMEDAY.

65

NEXT PROG ▶ DEVILS!

Nikolai Dante

THE ROMANOV DYNASTY

'It is much safer to be feared than loved.'
—NICCOLO MACHIAVELLI, WRITER, REFLECTING IN 1513 UPON THE COMPLEX NATURE OF CRUELTY AND MERCY.

'I've struck a little fear into the heart of the Empire and I've done plenty of loving; I know which one I prefer.'
—NIKOLAI DANTE, LOTHARIO AND ADVENTURER IN THE YEAR OF THE TSAR 2666... SPEAKING WITHOUT THINKING.

SCRIPT
ROBBIE MORRISON

ART
SIMON FRASER

COLOURS
ALISON KIRKPATRICK

LETTERS
ANNIE PARKHOUSE

RUDINSHTEIN. THE MOST ISOLATED FIEFDOM OF THE ROMANOV DYNASTY.

OOHHH!

GENTLEMEN.

THE LADY *ISN'T* FLATTERED BY YOUR ATTENTIONS.

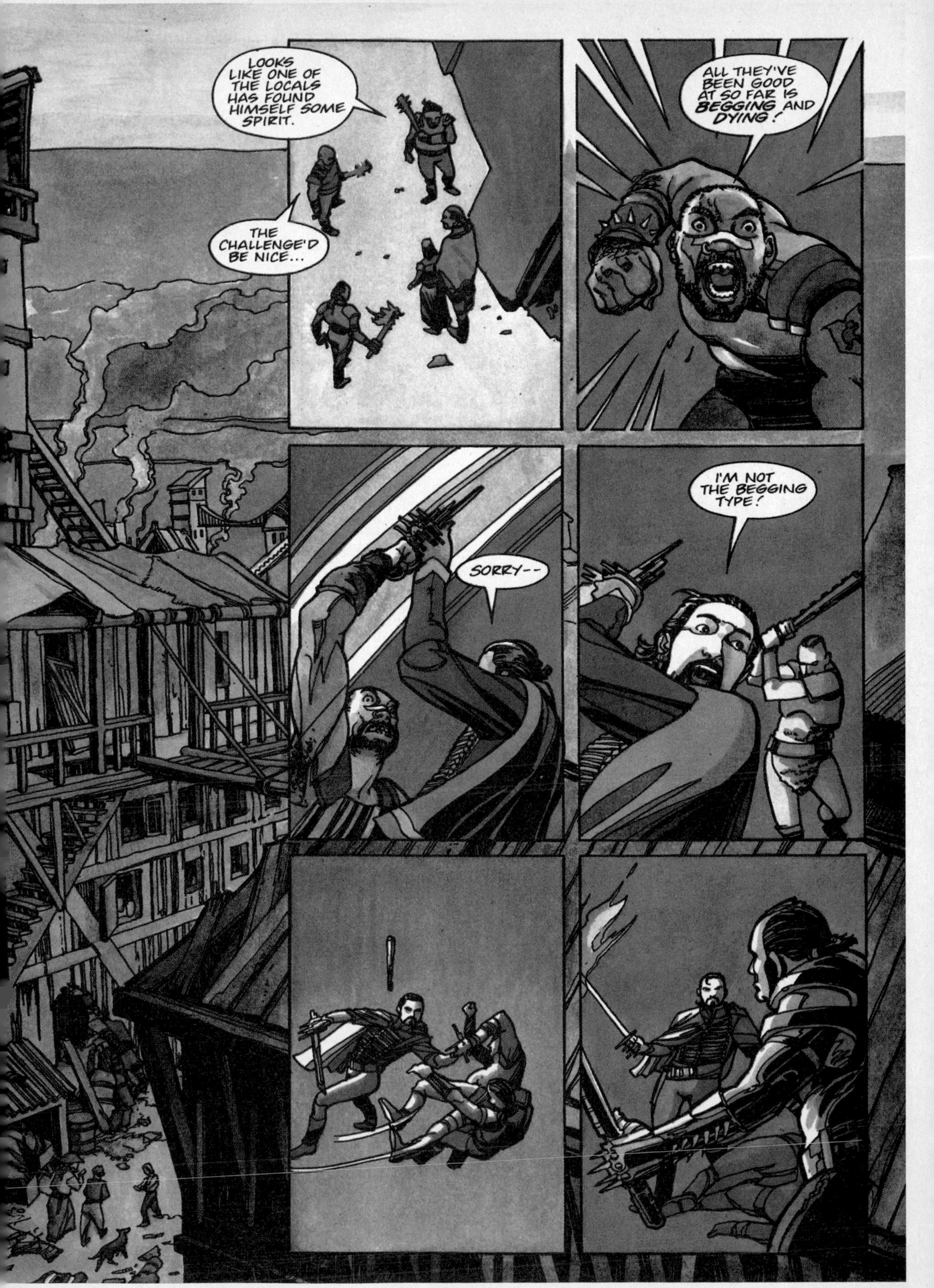
LOOKS LIKE ONE OF THE LOCALS HAS FOUND HIMSELF SOME SPIRIT.
THE CHALLENGE'D BE NICE...
ALL THEY'VE BEEN GOOD AT SO FAR IS BEGGING AND DYING!
SORRY--
I'M NOT THE BEGGING TYPE!
!

HHHLLLKKK!

YOU SHOULDN'T HAVE INTERFERED, STRANGER, NOT FOR ME.

THE KARAZIN ARE ANIMALS. THEY'LL HUNT YOU FOR THIS. THEY'LL KILL YOU.

KILL ME?

I'M TOO COOL TO KILL.

FORGIVE ME, SIRE! I DIDN'T SEE THE CREST! I DID NOT KNOW YOU WERE OF THE ROMANOV DYNASTY.

WHOA! GET UP— I'M NOT INTO HUMILITY.

THE NAME'S DANTE. NIKOLAI DANTE.

I'M THE BLACK SHEEP OF THE FAMILY.

THE WINTER PALACE OF THE ROMANOV DYNASTY. TWELVE HOURS PREVIOUSLY...

RUDINSHTEIN IS A GODFORSAKEN PART OF THE DYNASTY, OF NO STRATEGIC IMPORTANCE WHATSOEVER.

BUT *ANY* CHALLENGE TO OUR POWER, NO MATTER HOW MINOR, MUST BE CRUSHED.

THE *KARAZIN* WERE ONCE A NOBLE HOUSE LIKE OURSELVES. THE TSAR BROKE THEM THE WAY HE *LONGS* TO BREAK US.

THEY'VE LIVED AS OUTLAWS SINCE THE DESTRUCTION OF THEIR DYNASTY, SUPPORTING THEMSELVES BY PRODUCING AND DISTRIBUTING THE DRUG *CHERT-DEVIL*.

UNDER THEIR LEADER *LAZAREV*— AN ADDICT TO THE FRENZY OF CHERT— THEY'VE BECOME LITTLE MORE THAN *BARBARIANS*.

BUSINESS MUST BE BOOMING. THEY RECENTLY OVERWHELMED RUDINSHTEIN AND ENSLAVED THE POPULATION TO INCREASE CHERT PRODUCTION. WE DISPATCHED AN *ENVOY*, YOUNG *ARKADY*, TO OFFER THEM TERMS OF SURRENDER.

THEY RESPONDED BY TAKING HIM HOSTAGE. YOU WILL EFFECT HIS RESCUE AND INFORM US WHEN YOU ARE BOTH SAFE. *WE* WILL DO THE REST.

IT'S AN *HONOUR* TO BE CONSIDERED FOR SUCH A DANGEROUS MISSION, BUT I WAS HOPING TO MEET THE REST OF THE FAMILY.

YOU WILL, BOY.

YOU WILL.

69

THE KARAZIN REALLY TORE THIS PLACE APART.

THEIR BASE IS AT THE HEART OF THE CITY—**THEY HAVEN'T BEEN HERE.**

WHAT LITTLE MAINTENANCE THE GOVERNORS COULD AFFORD WAS CANCELLED WHEN THE ROMANOVS INCREASED THE YEARLY TRIBUTE.

HOW LONG HAVE YOU BEEN WITH THE ROMANOV DYNASTY?

ABOUT A **WEEK**—THOUGH IT FEELS MORE LIKE **TWELVE.**

YOU'RE NOT LIKE **THEM.**

IS THAT A **COMPLIMENT** OR AN **INSULT?**

I KNOW WHICH WAY I MEANT IT, SIRE.

MY HUSBAND AND FAMILY ARE AMONGST THE SLAVES TAKEN BY THE KARAZIN.

IF YOU WERE TO FREE THEM... I WOULD BE **YOURS.**

I KNOW THAT IS ALREADY YOUR **RIGHT** AS A MEMBER OF THE RULING DYNASTY, BUT—

THAT'S NO ONE'S RIGHT.

WHAT'S YOUR NAME, GIRL?

TAMARA.

I'LL FREE YOUR FAMILY, TAMARA. I'LL FREE **ALL** THE SLAVES.

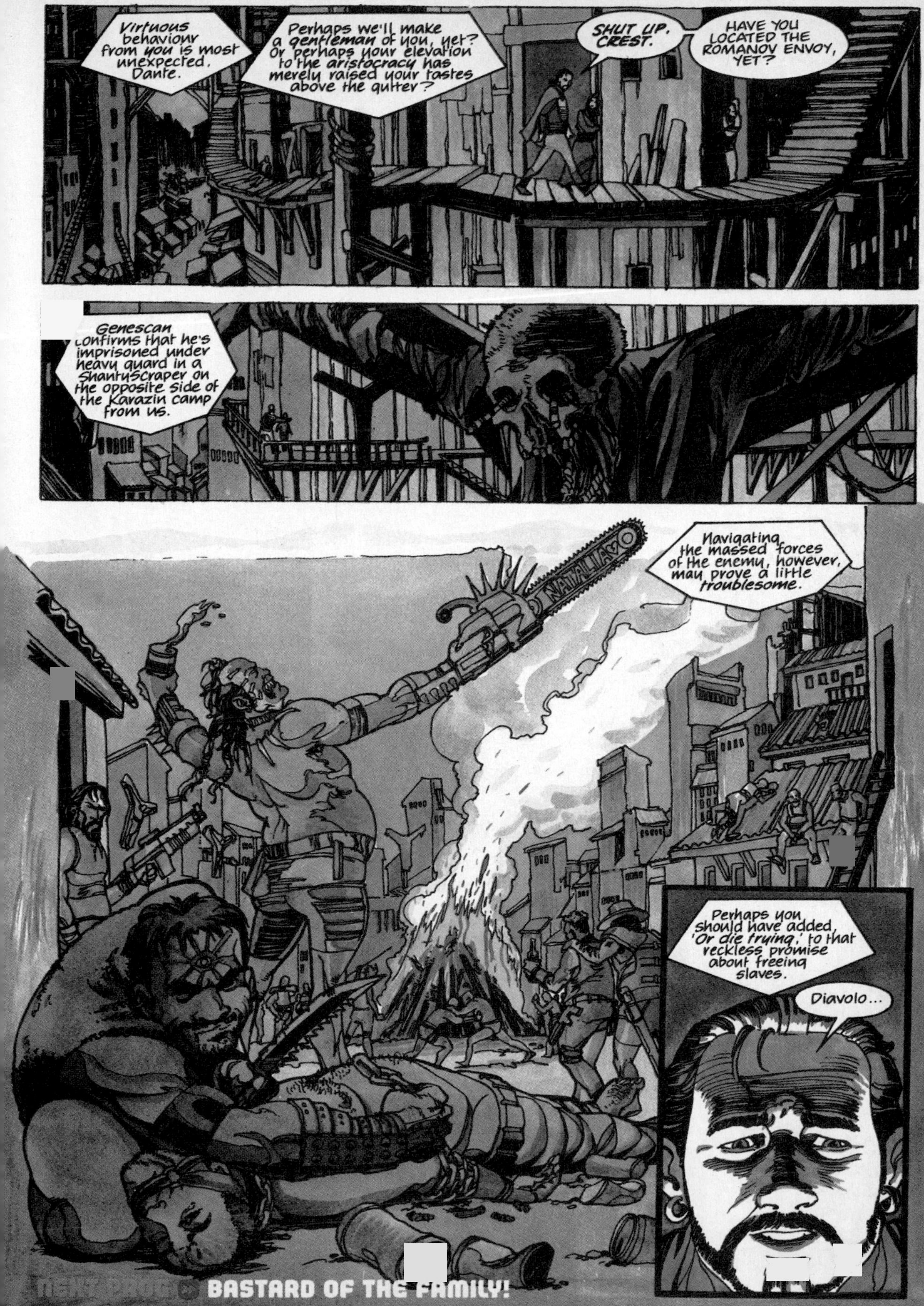
Virtuous behaviour from you is most unexpected, Dante.
Perhaps we'll make a gentleman of you, yet? Or perhaps your elevation to the aristocracy has merely raised your tastes above the gutter?
SHUT UP, CREST.
HAVE YOU LOCATED THE ROMANOV ENVOY, YET?
Genescan confirms that he's imprisoned under heavy guard in a ShantyScraper on the opposite side of the Karazin camp from us.
Navigating the massed forces of the enemy, however, may prove a little troublesome.
NATALIA
Perhaps you should have added, 'Or die trying,' to that reckless promise about freeing slaves.
Diavolo...
NEXT PROG BASTARD OF THE FAMILY!

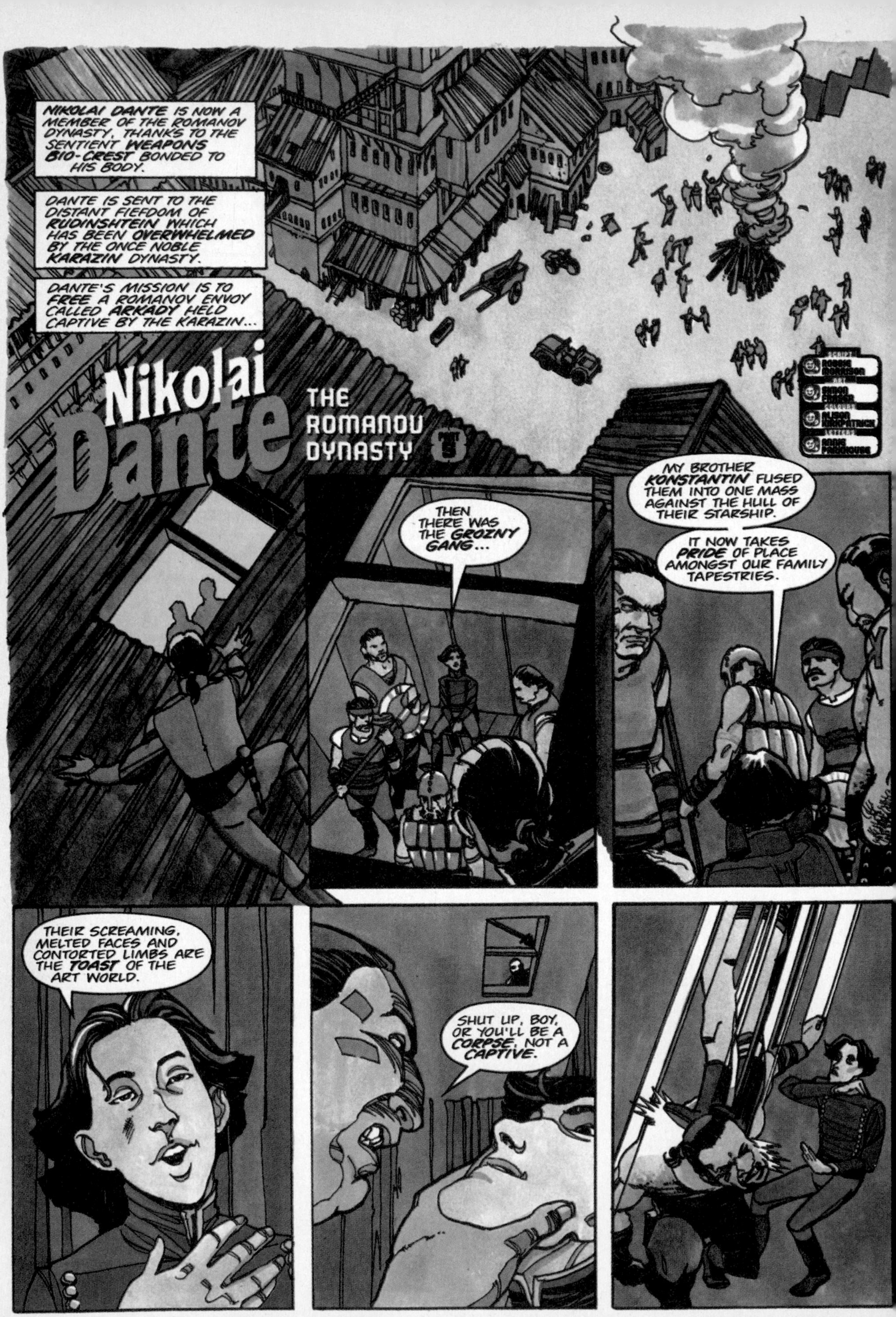
NIKOLAI DANTE IS NOW A MEMBER OF THE ROMANOV DYNASTY, THANKS TO THE SENTIENT WEAPONS BIO-CREST BONDED TO HIS BODY.
DANTE IS SENT TO THE DISTANT FIEFDOM OF RUDINSHTEIN WHICH HAS BEEN OVERWHELMED BY THE ONCE NOBLE KARAZIN DYNASTY.
DANTE'S MISSION IS TO FREE A ROMANOV ENVOY CALLED ARKADY HELD CAPTIVE BY THE KARAZIN...
Nikolai Dante
THE ROMANOV DYNASTY
THEN THERE WAS THE GROZNY GANG...
MY BROTHER KONSTANTIN FUSED THEM INTO ONE MASS AGAINST THE HULL OF THEIR STARSHIP.
IT NOW TAKES PRIDE OF PLACE AMONGST OUR FAMILY TAPESTRIES.
THEIR SCREAMING, MELTED FACES AND CONTORTED LIMBS ARE THE TOAST OF THE ART WORLD.
SHUT UP, BOY, OR YOU'LL BE A CORPSE, NOT A CAPTIVE.

FOR ALL THE *OSTENTATIOUS* METHODS OF ELIMINATING ENEMIES...

THE *SIMPLEST* ONES ARE SOMETIMES THE BEST.

For the record, Dante, I must state that I did *not* advise a frontal assault.

BACK-DOOR ENTRIES AREN'T MY STYLE, CREST.

YOU RESCUED ME FROM THE KARAZIN, BUT WHO'S GOING TO RESCUE *YOU* FROM *ME*?

73

YOU BEAR THE CREST UNDER *FALSE* PRETENCES, STRANGER.

I WAS TO HAVE RECEIVED MY BIRTHRIGHT WEAPONS CREST BEFORE COMING HERE. SOMEONE— *YOU*—INTERCEPTED IT IN TRANSIT.

THIS WAS TO HAVE BEEN MY FIRST MISSION FOR THE DYNASTY. *FIRST BLOOD.*

I SHOULD KILL YOU FOR *ROBBING* ME OF THAT HONOUR.

WHOOMPH!

YOU'VE *HAD* YOUR FIRST BLOOD...

AND IF YOU WANT TO TRY SPILLING MINE *GET IN LINE!*

THERE'S A *CITY FULL* OF THIEVES AND MURDERERS OUT THERE WAITING TO DO THE SAME...

LAZAREV!

LAZAREV!

THE *ENTERTAINMENT'S* ABOUT TO COMMENCE...

WHAT?

'EACH NIGHT, *LAZAREV,* THE KARAZIN LEADER, FORCES SLAVES TO ENGAGE HIM IN COMBAT!'

LAZAREV!

LAZAREV!

74

I'M GIVING YOU AN OPPORTUNITY YOU DON'T *DESERVE.*

LIVE LIKE *SLAVES* — OR *DIE* LIKE FREE MEN.

WEAPONS.

CHERT.

GGRRRAAAA

LAZAREV'S ADDICTED TO *CHERT*, THE DRUG THE KARAZIN MANUFACTURE.

THE *DUELS* FEED HIS HABIT, SPEEDING THE DRUG'S PROGRESS THROUGH HIS SYSTEM.

'THERE'S NOTHING LIKE THE *THRILL OF THE KILL* TO GET THE BLOOD PUMPING.'

GIVE THE ORDER TO ATTACK *NOW*.

I WANT TO WATCH SOME *REAL* BLOOD-SPORTS.

NO! WE HAVE TO FREE THE SLAVES FIRST.

WHAT!? WE DON'T FIGHT FOR *THEM*. THEY FIGHT FOR *US*.

THEY'RE *OURS* TO DO WITH AS WE PLEASE.

I MADE A *PROMISE*.

GET YOURSELF TO SAFETY AND GIVE ME TWENTY MINUTES, THEN ORDER THE ATTACK.

PROMISES ARE FOR *BREAKING*.

ARKADY ROMANOV TO DYNASTY COMMAND. LAUNCH *EAGLESTRIKE* NOW.

AND THEY CALL *ME* THE *BASTARD* OF THE FAMILY!

PLEASE, LORD LAZAREV! MY *HUSBAND*— DON'T KILL HIM!

I CAN *HELP* YOU...

THERE'S A ROMANOV IN YOUR CAMP. HE *FORCED* ME TO LEAD HIM HERE.

ONCE HE FREES THEIR ENVOY, THEY'LL LAUNCH A *MAJOR* ATTACK.

YOU LED A *ROMANOV* TO ME AND DARE TO ASK FOR *MERCY*!?

THERE! HEADING FOR THE *SLAVE PENS!*

GET OUT OF HERE!

I'LL HOLD THEM FOR AS LONG AS I CAN!

KILL HIM!

BRING ME HIS HEAD!

NEXT PROG ▷ MORE ABOUT THE ART OF DIPLOMACY!

SCRIPT
ROBBIE MORRISON
ART
SIMON FRASER
COLOURS
ALISON KIRKPATRICK
LETTERS
ANNIE PARKHOUSE

NIKOLAI DANTE IS IN THE DISTANT ROMANOV FIEFDOM OF RUDINSHTEIN, WHICH HAS BEEN OVERWHELMED BY THE DRUG-DEALING, DECADENT KARAZIN DYNASTY.

DANTE RESCUES A ROMANOV ENVOY AND FREES THE KARAZIN SLAVES BUT THEIR ESCAPE IS BLOCKED...

TAKE THE ROMANOV FIRST!

Nikolai Dante
THE ROMANOV DYNASTY
PART 6

THE NAME'S DANTE!

HUSH, CHILD.

IF YOU MISS YOUR LOVER THAT MUCH, I'LL HAPPILY SEND YOU TO JOIN HIM!

GGGNNHH!

Dante! The odds against surviving this unnecessary encounter are astronomical!

QUOTE ME ODDS WHEN I'M GAMBLING WITH *MONEY*, CREST!

NOT WITH MY *LIFE!*

UUUHH!

YOU'VE A TALENT FOR TROUBLE, LITTLE BROTHER.

IF WE WERE ALL LIKE *YOU*, THE ROMANOVS WOULD BE A *VERY* SHORT-LIVED DYNASTY.

SAY *HELLO* TO THE REST OF THE FAMILY— AND *FAREWELL* TO THE KARAZIN.

FROM THE FILES OF THE RAVEN CORPS:

KONSTANTIN: Sophisticated and Charming. A born leader. A born killer. A born everything.
CREST CAPABILITIES: The ability to generate fusion energy comparable to the greatest Imperial war machines from within his own body.

LULU: A terrifying seductive beauty who has driven the strongest Imperial subjects to suicide and insanity.
CREST CAPABILITIES: The creation of cybernetic entities which devour their prey in insect-like swarms.

Fuoco...

VIKTOR: The lone wolf of the Romanovs. Dwells in isolation, shunning even the company of his siblings unless necessary.
CREST CAPABILITIES: Unknown. No Imperial agent has ever dared investigate him.

ANDREAS: Incorrigible adventurer and philandering seducer of Widows and Heiresses.
CREST CAPABILITIES: Bio-blades which generate an energy-field of variable size. Rumoured to have once decapitated 27 men with a single blade.

NASTASIA: The Romanov Bitch. Narcissistic and coquettish. Habitual killer of anyone less admiring of her looks than she is herself.
CREST CAPABILITIES: The transmutation of bodily fluids into venomous or acidic substances.

THIS IS *NOT* A PROPOSITION, LAZAREV—YOU HAVE NO CHOICE IN THE MATTER.

CONTINUE CHERT PRODUCTION, BUT HAND OVER *ALL* PROFITS TO US. IN RETURN, YOU WILL BE GIVEN RUDINSHTEIN TO *RULE* AS YOU SEE FIT.

Tamara...

I TOLD YOU IT WOULD BE *FUN* TO WATCH...

NO!

LOOK WHAT HE DID TO THESE PEOPLE! YOU CAN'T JUST GIVE THEM TO HIM!

LORD KONSTANTIN, I PLEDGE *UNDYING* LOYALTY TO THE ROMANOV DYNASTY.

THAT'S THE *SPIRIT.*

IT'S CALLED *DIPLOMACY.*

RUDINSHTEIN FEARS *LAZAREV,* LAZAREV FEARS *US*—WHAT *BETTER* WAY TO KEEP *ORDER?*

DIPLOMACY... I'LL HAVE TO LEARN THAT SOMEDAY.

YOU'VE INSULTED MY HONOUR! I DEMAND SATISFACTION THROUGH--

DO YOU, UH, MIND IF I?

NOT AT ALL! FEEL FREE.

WEAPONS. CHERT.

DANTE!

NEXT PROG ◉ HEROES DIE YOUNG...

Evasive action, Dante! Evasive action!

RELAX CREST, I'VE GOT HIS MEASURE...

NIKOLAI DANTE IS IN THE DISTANT ROMANOV FIEFDOM OF *RUDINSHTEIN*, A POOR PROVINCE CONTROLLED BY THE DRUG-DEALING, DECADENT *KARAZIN* DYNASTY.

DANTE IS FIGHTING A DUEL TO THE DEATH WITH THE KARAZIN LEADER LAZAREV. THE BATTLE IS WATCHED BY DANTE'S ROMANOV SIBLINGS...

Nikolai Dante

THE ROMANOV DYNASTY

WWOOAARRGH!

Fool!

Lazarev is addicted to Chert, the most powerful stimulative substance known to humanity. It raises psycho-physical sensations to an orgiastic frenzy!

GIVE ME THAT IN SCUMBAG LANGUAGE...

He enjoys pain!

AAAGH-KKK!!

His strike fractured every rib on your left side — shield yourself from further attack.

EA-EASY FOR YOU TO SAY...

SCRIPT
ROBBIE MORRISON
ART
SIMON FRASER
COLOURS
ALISON KIRKPATRICK
LETTERS
ANNIE PARKHOUSE

Dante...

I KNOW! I KNOW!

EVASIVE ACTION!

Evasive action usually means getting yourself out of danger, not *deeper* into it...

OOHFFF!

AKK!?

I THINK WE GOT HIM, CREST...

HEH.

I think not...

GGRRRAAAA!

HAAAH!

HUHH!?

PAINFUL ENOUGH?

STILL ENJOYING YOURSELF?

HEH HEH HEH

GRRAAAAaaakkk!!

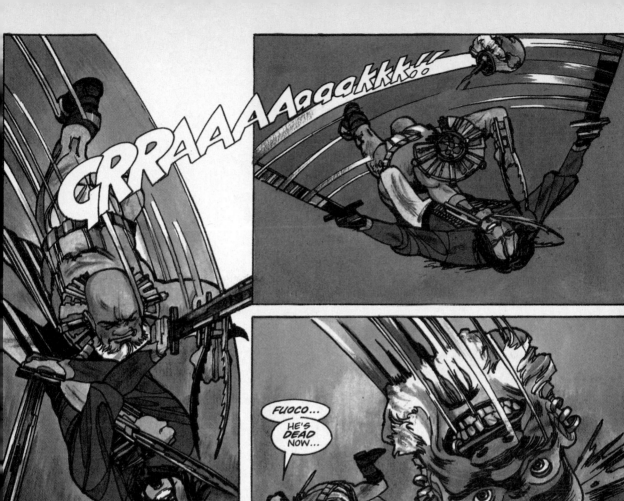

FUOCO...
HE'S DEAD
NOW...

Famous last words, thief...

Now why couldn't you have done that at the very start?

cough... shut up, crest...

87

I'D SAY OUR BASTARD BROTHER PULLED THAT OFF WITH A CERTAIN AMOUNT OF *CRUDE STYLE*.

HE *MOANS* WELL. I PREFER A MAN TO *WHIMPER*, BUT *HE MOANS* WELL.

SURELY IT'S *KINDEST* TO KILL HIM NOW — SAVE THE DYNASTY *FURTHER* EMBARRASSMENT.

KONSTANTIN? KILL HIM?

IT MIGHT NOT BE THAT EASY.

DANTE! DANTE! DANTE!

WHEN WAS THE LAST TIME ANYONE CHEERED FOR THE ROMANOV DYNASTY WITHOUT A *GUN* AT THEIR HEAD?

SOMETIMES IT *PAYS* TO HAVE A *HERO* IN THE FAMILY.

WHAT DO *YOU* SAY TO THAT, *LITTLE BROTHER?*

HEROES BE DAMNED...

NEXT PROG ▷ PATERNAL INSTINCTS!

THE ROMANOV WINTER PALACE, WHERE NIKOLAI DANTE IS NURSING THE WOUNDS SUFFERED DURING HIS FIRST MISSION AS THE NEW MEMBER OF THE ROMANOV DYNASTY...

AAOOWWW!

Nikolai Dante

THE ROMANOV DYNASTY

PART 8

SCRIPT
ROBBIE MORRISON

ART
SIMON FRASER

COLOURS
ALISON KIRKPATRICK

LETTERS
ANNIE PARKHOUSE

WHOA! WHOA!

COULD YOU MOVE OVER JUST A LITTLE?

THIS IS SILLY— I TOLD YOU YOU WEREN'T UP TO IT, YET.

UP TO IT? IF WE CAN GET IT TOGETHER JUST A LITTLE BIT MORE...

YOU'LL FIND THAT'S FAR FROM THE CASE...

OOOHH!

HUHH!?

WHOA!

BY ANASTASIA'S BONES! THE UNIT GYROSCOPE—

—IS UNDER *MY* CONTROL, GIRL.

GET OUT. FROM NOW ON YOUNG NIKOLAI WILL BE ATTENDED *ONLY* BY *MALE* MEDICS.

YES, LORD DMITRI.

WHEN YOU CAME TO US, I TOLD YOU THAT BEARING THE CREST AND BEING *WORTHY* OF IT WERE ENTIRELY DIFFERENT THINGS.

I'M BEGINNING TO WONDER WHETHER YOU EVEN *WANT* TO BE WORTHY...

YOU INITIATED A DUEL WITH LAZAREV IN DEFIANCE OF A DYNASTIC DECREE TO INSTALL HIM AS PUPPET GOVERNOR OF RUDINSHTEIN. *WHY?*

HE WOULD HAVE *DESTROYED* THEM. HE WAS A TYRANT, A BARBARIAN...

MANY SAY THE SAME OF ME.

I VIEW IT AS *COMPLIMENTARY*, A TESTAMENT TO ROMANOV POWER AND AUTHORITY.

I DID IT FOR *POWER*...

TO PROVE I'M *MORE* THAN JUST THE *BASTARD SON* OF THE ROMANOV DYNASTY.

PROVE IT TO *WHO? YOURSELF?* TO PROVE YOU'RE *BETTER* THAN *US*, PERHAPS?

SINCE WINNING RUDINSHTEIN, YOU'VE *LOWERED* THEIR TAXES, INTRODUCED *BENEFICIAL* REFORMS...

LOWERING THEIR TAXES LETS THEM GENERATE NEW WEALTH, GIVES THEM STABILITY AND SECURITY.

EVERYBODY SAYS I'M A THIEF— I'LL *ROB THEM BLIND* LATER.

NEVER LET THEM *LOVE* YOU— IT'S *EASY* TO HURT THE THINGS YOU LOVE.

MAKE THEM *FEAR* YOU. FEAR IS THE KEY.

HEY...

I CAN BE *SCARY*...

NO, BOY, YOU *CAN'T!*

YOU *DON'T* HAVE THE *KILLING* IN YOU!

AND *WITHOUT* THE KILLING, YOU'RE ONLY FIT *FOR* KILLING!

WHY DO YOU THINK I'M HERE?

IT'S *JUDGMENT DAY*, YOUNG NIKOLAI.

SHAME REALLY. I'VE GROWN FOND OF YOUR UNPREDICTABILITY IN THE WAY A HORSEMAN FEELS TOWARDS A STEED HE MUST BREAK.

SADLY, UNPREDICTABILITY IN THE RANKS IS SOMETHING *NO* IMPERIAL DYNASTY CAN AFFORD.

THE *THIEVES' WORLD* HAS LEFT ITS MARK ON YOU. I THINK YOU'RE TOO MUCH YOUR OWN MAN TO EVER BE TRUSTED.

PERHAPS IF WE'D HAD YOU SINCE *BIRTH...*

HOW IS YOUR *MOTHER?* I KNOW YOU'VE BEEN CHECKING DYNASTY RECORDS TO SEE WHICH OF US KNEW HER.

STILL *REIVING* THE EMPIRE FOR ALL SHE'S WORTH?

I HAVEN'T SEEN HER IN OVER *10* YEARS.

SHE *ABANDONED* ME...

SHE WAS QUITE A WOMAN. FIERY, ARROGANT, TREACHEROUS...

I HAD TO *BREAK* HER IN SOME WAY...

WHAT?

YOU DIDN'T THINK YOU WERE CONCEIVED OUT OF *LOVE,* DID YOU?

93

BASTARD!

I'M AFRAID YOU'RE THE ONLY ONE THAT INSULT APPLIES TO...

ALL ROMANOVS BEAR THE CREST...

YOU THINK I'D GIVE THAT PACK OF WOLVES I SIRED WEAPONS THEY CAN DESTROY ME WITH?

THE KILLING'S IN YOU NOW, ISN'T IT, BOY!

LEARN TO LOVE IT IF YOU WANT TO LIVE!

THAT'S WHAT IT MEANS TO BE PART OF THE ROMANOV DYNASTY.

THE DYNASTY IS EVERYTHING AND I AM THE DYNASTY!

YOU'LL HAVE TO KILL AT MY COMMAND. WITHOUT PROVOCATION.

FRIENDS, ENEMIES, LOVERS, YOU'LL KILL THEM ALL IN THE NAME OF ROMANOV!

STILL THINK YOU'RE WORTHY, YOUNG NIKOLAI?

CAN YOU ACCEPT THE KILLING!?

...KILL YOU...

I'LL KILL YOU...

HA HA HA HA HA!

YOU WOULD IF YOU COULD. ALL MY CHILDREN WOULD. I BRED IT INTO THEM.

RUTHLESSNESS. AMBITION. THAT'S WHAT GIVES US OUR POWER, MAKES THE TSAR FEAR US. NOT THE WEAPONS CRESTS.

REST EASY, NIKOLAI DANTE. WE'LL MAKE A ROMANOV OUT OF YOU, YET.

BOJEMOI...

WELCOME TO THE FAMILY...

THE END

RUSSIA'S GREATEST LOVE MACHINE

Script: Robbie Morrison

Art: Chris Weston

Letters: Annie Parkhouse

Originally published in *2000 AD* Prog 1066

Nikolai Dante

Russia's Greatest Love Machine

script: ROBBIE MORRISON

art: SPACEBOY

letters: ANNIE PARKHOUSE

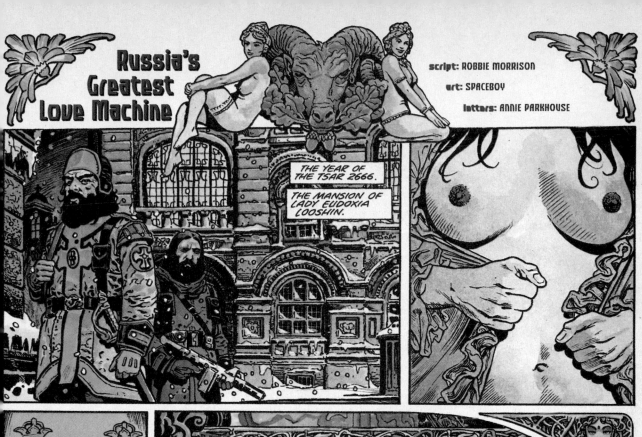

THE YEAR OF THE TSAR 2666.

THE MANSION OF LADY EUDOXIA LOOSHIN.

HMMM...

NICE BEARD!

THANK YOU.

I TRIM IT MYSELF.

...e Devil's Martyrs are an Imperial Cult fanatically devoted to the hedonistic Grigori Rasputin, the infamous Mad Monk, whose corrupt influence over the last Tsar of the First Empire contributed to its downfall many centuries ago.

Sex with the Devil's Martyrs is reputed to be an experience of the wildest excess.

Lady Eudoxia Looshin, a disciple of legendary decadence, has waylaid Nikolai Dante with the intention of testing his ladykiller reputation to the limit.

My morally deficient 'master' would normally relish the challenge, however, as a sign of devotion to the hirsute Rasputin, all Devil's Martyrs sport beards — even the women.

KISS ME, NIKOLAI!

Thick, full, heavy, manly beards.

KISS ME!

WHOA! WHOA! SORRY!

I, UH, JUST NEED TO GO TO THE TOILET! DESPERATELY!

98

GET A GRIP OF YOURSELF!

SHE'S A BEAUTIFUL WOMAN! *BEAUTIFUL, BUXOM, SWEET* AND *SEXY*—JUST A WEE BIT *HAIRY.*

Surely you don't judge beauty on a depilatory scale? A man of your experience must have been with hirsute women before.

ARMPITS, FINE! LEGS, WHAT THE HELL! BUT, BUT— SHE'S GOT A *BUSHIER BEARD* THAN ME!

Her beard has obviously awakened your homophobia. Or perhaps something deeper?

Perhaps you're scared you'll enjoy it? If you can kiss a bearded woman, why not a man?

IF YOU WEREN'T *BONDED* TO ME, CREST, I'D RUN YOU THROUGH FOR THAT!

I'M *HETERO* FROM *HEAD* TO *TOE*—AND I'LL *PROVE* IT!

GET READY FOR SOME *LOVING,* MILADY!

I'M COMING IN *HOT* AND *HARD!*

AHH, DANTÉ?

I SEE YOU'VE INTRODUCED YOURSELF TO MY BUTLER, IVAN.

GOOD EVENING, SIR.

EEUCH!

IT MIGHT BE PRUDENT IF I LEFT NOW, MADAM.

YOU MAY FEEL THE NEED OF THIS, SIR.

EXAGGERATED, MILADY!? I'M COOLER THAN CASANOVA AND RANDIER THAN RASPUTIN.'

WHEN THE DEVIL'S MARTYRS ARE DEAD AND BURIED, DANTE'S DISCIPLES'LL STILL BE HAVING A HELL OF A TIME!

I'M DISAPPOINTED, NIKOLAI.

YOUR REPUTATION AS A LADIES' MAN SEEMS TO HAVE BEEN EXAGGERATED. I'D HAVE THOUGHT YOU MORE OPEN-MINDED.

AS FOR OPEN-MINDED, I JUST SNOGGED YOUR BUTLER!

I FINALLY GET YOU WHERE I WANT YOU.

YEAH, LET'S GET IT ON AND BUMP SOME BRISTLES TOGETHER.

WEIRD HOW YOUR BEARD *ITCHES* DURING MOMENTS OF PASSION...

MUST BE ALL THAT *STATIC* ELECTRICITY...

RA-RA-RASPUTIN, RUSSIA'S GREATEST LOVE MACHINE, THERE WAS A CAT WHO REALLY WAS COOL.

Are you always so happy creeping out of ladies' bedchambers like a thief in the night?

LOVE 'EM AND LEAVE 'EM, CREST, THAT'S THE WAY OF THE THIEVES' WORLD— AND RELIEVE THEM OF THEIR *JEWELLRY* TOO, IF YOU CAN.

BESIDES, I COULDN'T LAST ANOTHER 10 ROUNDS, MY FACE IS *KILLING* ME.

IT'S USUALLY *ME* WHO LEAVES *GIRLS* WITH *STUBBLE BURNS!*

THE END

THE GENTLEMAN THIEF

Script: Robbie Morrison

Art: Simon Fraser

Colors: Alison Kirkpatrick

Letters: Annie Parkhouse

Originally published in *2000 AD* Progs 1067-1070

SCRIPT
ROBBIE MORRISON
ART
SIMON FRASER
COLOURS
ALISON KIRKPATRICK
LETTERS
ANNIE PARKHOUSE

Nikolai Dante

THE GENTLEMAN THIEF PART 1

HOTEL YALTA, PLEASURE RESORT OF THE IMPERIAL ARISTOCRACY, STRETCHING ALONG THE ENTIRE COASTLINE OF THE BLACK SEA.

YOU'VE ARRIVED JUST IN TIME, *COUNTESSA DE WINTER*. ONE OF OUR OTHER GUESTS IS THROWING THE MOST *INCREDIBLE* PARTY.

YOUR *USUAL* SUITE?

NO.

SOMETHING A LITTLE *LARGER* THIS TIME. SPARE NO LUXURY.

I WANT IT *ALL.*

YOU GAVE THE FLOOR TRADITIONALLY RESERVED FOR MY OFFICERS AND I TO *ONE MAN*? A *WHOLE FLOOR*!?

THE GUEST WAS *MOST* INSISTENT, CAPTAIN. HE SAID THE ROOMS WERE TOO GOOD TO *WASTE* ON THE TSAR'S SOLDIERS.

WHERE IS THIS *UPSTART*?

IN THE *GAMBLING* SECTOR. JUST FOLLOW THE *CROWDS.*

BOJEMOI!

YOU DON'T THINK IT'S A TRIFLE *OSTENTATIOUS*, DO YOU?

ON THE CONTRARY, I THINK THEY'RE *MAGNIFICENT*.

I WAS TALKING ABOUT MY TATTOO.

I KNOW.

SIR! THE HOTEL SEEMS TO HAVE MADE A MISTAKE. *YOU* ARE OCCUPYING *OUR* ROOMS, THOUGH I'M SURE YOU'LL SOON VACATE THEM IN THE NAME OF THE TSAR.

MISTAKE? I DOUBT IT.

ROOMS AT THE YALTA ARE USUALLY ALLOCATED BY THE *SIZE OF A MAN'S POUCH.*

MONEY POUCH, THAT IS.

I WOULDN'T WANT TO MAKE YOU FEEL ANY MORE *INADEQUATE* THAN YOU ALREADY ARE.

WHAT'S YOUR NAME, YOU *ARROGANT SWINE?*

DANTE.

NIKOLAI DANTE.

I'M *CAPTAIN ARBATOV* OF THE *TSAR'S LIGHTHORSEMEN.*

ONE OF MY BROTHERS WAS *SKINNED ALIVE* BECAUSE OF YOU, ANOTHER *HURLED* FROM THE WINTER PALACE.

IT'S A PLEASURE TO MAKE YOUR *ACQUAINTANCE!*

Y'KNOW, CAPTAIN...

YOUR FAMILY AND I ARE GOING TO HAVE TO *STOP* MEETING LIKE THIS...

IT'S BAD FOR YOUR *HEALTH!*

YOU'LL PAY FOR THAT, *ROMANOV DOG!*

COOL!

THE ONLY THING THE PARTY'S MISSING IS A GOOD *BRAWL!*

HALT! ANY FURTHER AGGRESSION WILL BE REPAID IN KIND!

THE HOTEL YALTA IS *NEUTRAL TERRITORY*, GENTLEMEN, FREE OF IMPERIAL DISPUTES OR DYNASTIC INTRIGUE— *BY ORDER OF THE TSAR.*

WE ARE *BUSINESSMEN*, AND *ANYTHING* OR *ANYONE* DISRUPTING BUSINESS WILL NOT BE TOLERATED.

BUT, *LORD KONIGSBERG,* DANTE—

ULIURRKK!

ANYTHING OR ANYONE, CAPTAIN. YOU AND YOUR MEN WILL BE GIVEN OTHER ROOMS. DO *NOT* ABUSE OUR HOSPITALITY AGAIN.

A WORD OF ADVICE TO THE *HIGH SPENDERS* AMONGST YOU.

THE YALTA INDULGES YOUR *EVERY* PLEASURE, BUT *ALWAYS* REMEMBER OUR MOTTO...

NO ONE HERE GETS OUT ALIVE WITHOUT PAYING THEIR BILL...

NIKOLAI DANTE.

YOU HAVE A COMMUNICATION FROM *THE WINTER PALACE.*

PROBABLY THE FAMILY TELLING ME TO SPEND *MORE* MONEY—THEY MUST BE EMBARRASSED AT HOW *CHEAPLY* I'M LIVING.

LULU! YOU'RE LOOKING ESPECIALLY *VAMPISH* TODAY!

HOW'RE THINGS BACK AT THE *HUMBLE* FAMILY HOME?

ALL THE BETTER FOR YOUR *ABSENCE*, LITTLE BROTHER. *SHAME* THEY CAN'T STAY THAT WAY.

THE WINTER PALACE OF THE ROMANOV DYNASTY.

THE TSAR HAS ORDERED A GATHERING OF THE IMPERIAL HOUSES. RETURN HERE WITHIN THE WEEK.

I HOPE YOU DON'T HAVE TROUBLE SETTLING YOUR BILL.

TROUBLE? WITH THE RICHES OF THE ROMANOV DYNASTY BEHIND ME?

DIDN'T ANYONE TELL YOU?

THE WEALTH OF THE ROMANOV ELITE IS *DEPENDENT* ON THE LANDS THEY GOVERN. WHATEVER *YOU* SPEND IS DEDUCTED FROM RUDINSHTEIN'S FINANCES.

BUT RUDINSHTEIN'S THE *POOREST* CITY IN THE EMPIRE.

YES, I HOPE YOU HAVEN'T BEEN *TOO* EXTRAVAGANT. IF RUDINSHTEIN IS BANKRUPTED, ITS INHABITANTS WILL BE SENT TO A *GULAG* TO REPAY THE DEBT *YOU*'VE BURDENED THEM WITH.

LULU, uh, YOU COULDN'T *LEND* ME—

DON'T BE *SILLY.* LIKE YOU SAID, I'M A *VAMP*—I SEDUCE WEAK-WILLED ROMANTICS LIKE YOU AND *TAKE* THEIR MONEY.

GOODBYE.

Fuoco...

SOMETHING *AMISS,* DANTE'?

NOT AT ALL.

MORE WINE! FOR EVERYBODY!

Not a wise move considering your financial position, Dante.

LET'S KEEP THEM SPILLING *WINE* JUST NOW, *CREST.*

THEY'LL BE AFTER MY *BLOOD* SOON ENOUGH...

NEXT PROG ▷ THE ▮ARK ▮F ▮▮NTE

HOTEL YALTA, ON THE COAST OF THE BLACK SEA.

THE BEDCHAMBER OF COUNTESSA DE WINTER.

THANK YOU FOR ESCORTING ME TO MY SUITE, GENERAL, AND FOR YOUR RIVETING REPARTEE THIS EVENING, BUT IT MIGHT BE BETTER IF YOU RETURNED TO YOUR OWN ROOMS.

SCRIPT: ROBBIE MORRISON
ART: SIMON FRASER
COLOURS: ALISON KIRKPATRICK
LETTERS: ANNIE PARKHOUSE

RETREAT, MY DEAR COUNTESSA!?

I, GENERAL SHITOV, DO NOT KNOW THE MEANING OF THE WORD — NOT EVEN AFTER FACING THE CABINET NOIRE AT THE BATTLE OF BUKHARA.

FIX BAYONETS AND CHARGE, I SAY.

FIX BAYONETS AND CHARGE!

YOUR MONEY OR YOUR LIFE!

'The incorrigible Nikolai Dante found himself penniless in the Hotel Yalta, whose motto, "No one here gets out alive without paying their bill," was brutally enforced.'

'There was only one option — thievery.'
FROM 'BRIGANDS OF THE EMPIRE,' BY MARIA BERIA.

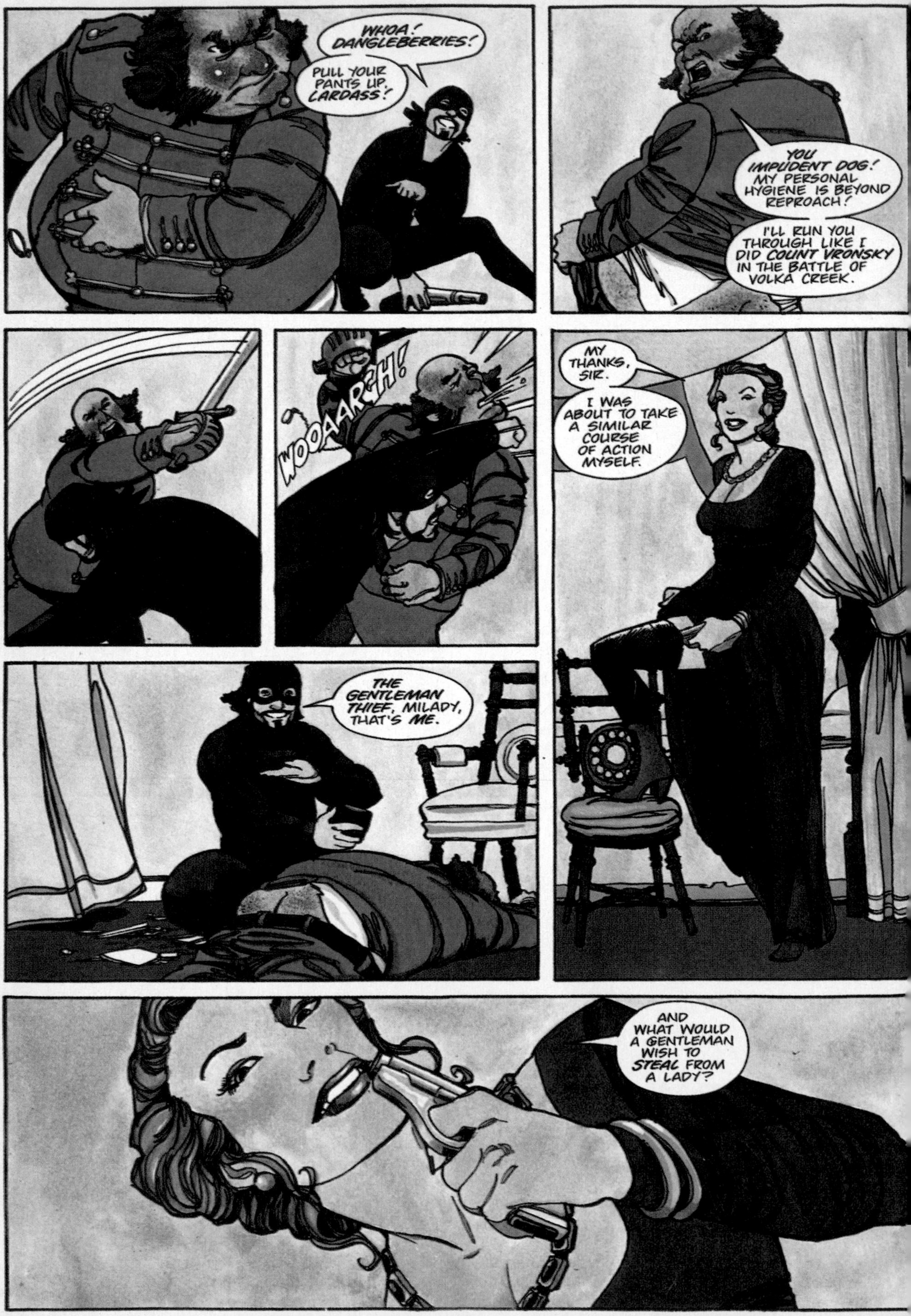
WHOA! DANGLEBERRIES!
PULL YOUR PANTS UP, LARDASS!
YOU IMPUDENT DOG! MY PERSONAL HYGIENE IS BEYOND REPROACH!
I'LL RUN YOU THROUGH LIKE I DID COUNT VRONSKY IN THE BATTLE OF VOLKA CREEK.
WOOAARGH!
MY THANKS, SIR.
I WAS ABOUT TO TAKE A SIMILAR COURSE OF ACTION MYSELF.
THE GENTLEMAN THIEF, MILADY, THAT'S ME.
AND WHAT WOULD A GENTLEMAN WISH TO STEAL FROM A LADY?

ONLY A *KISS* FROM THOSE *SWEET* LIPS.

I SHOULD WEAR A MASK MORE OFTEN, IT WORKS *WONDERS* WITH THE LADIES.

THAT'S THE *TENTH* SET OF TONSILS I'VE TICKLED TONIGHT, THOUGH THEY WERE DEFINITELY THE *TASTIEST.*

'The Hotel *Yalta* is definitely the place to be. In addition to an ongoing party of epic magnitude, it has become the target of a daring Gentleman Thief.'

'In just a few short days, the brigand has set the public imagination racing and earned himself a small fortune...

'...not to mention an astronomical price on his head, courtesy of the *Yalta's* enraged owners.' — *THE IMPERIAL TIMES.*

BOJEMOI!

CREST!

YOU'RE SUPPOSED TO BE DISRUPTING THEIR SCANNERS SO THEY CAN'T FIND ME!

I am, but I can't make you invisible.

If you insist on massaging your ego by hanging around posing in plain sight, how can they possibly *not* find you?

'The Thief delights in goading his pursuers into spectacular rooftop pursuits, then vanishes like a phantom just when capture seems inevitable!'
— THE IMPERIAL TIMES.

GUNHAWK 7 TO YALTA COMMAND. WE'VE LOST HIM — AGAIN!

YOU RANDY ROGUE!

'Noblewomen from all over the Empire are rumoured to be journeying to the Yalta in the hope of having their favours stolen by this dashing adventurer.'— *THE IMPERIAL TIMES.*

YOU'VE COME TO *RAVISH* ME, HAVEN'T YOU, SIR. RAVISH ME AND *STEAL* MY MONEY.

THE MONEY WOULD BE FINE, AS FOR THE RAVISHING...

IT'S BEEN A *LONG* NIGHT, I DON'T KNOW IF I'M *UP* TO IT.

UP TO IT!

YOU'VE A *WICKED TONGUE* YOU *BAWDY* FELLOW!

I'LL DEFEND MY MONEY AS *VALIANTLY* AS MY *HONOUR*—YOU'LL HAVE TO *TAKE* THEM FROM ME.

JANGLE!

IT'S ALRIGHT, *REALLY*. KEEP THEM. I'LL BE OFF.

JINGLE!

YOU CAN'T TRICK ME, YOU *SCOUNDREL*. YOU'VE BEEN *UNDRESSING* ME WITH YOUR EYES SINCE YOU ARRIVED!

SHAMELESSLY *CARESSING* MY *RIPE* FLESH WITH THEM.

UH. *OVER-RIPE*, ACTUALLY. FIT TO *BURST*, IN FACT.

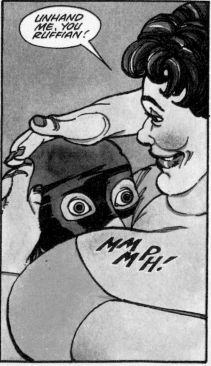

UNHAND ME, YOU *RUFFIAN!*

MMPH!

I'M NOT SOME *TAME* STEED YOU CAN *CASUALLY MOUNT!*

BOJEMOI!

OH, YOU DIRTY DEVIL! YOU RANDY ROGUE!

WHOA! WHOA!

THERE'S GOT TO BE EASIER WAYS OF MAKING A DISHONEST LIVING.

For once, Dante, I agree.

Isn't a more surreptitious return to your rooms warranted bearing in mind the situation?

GIVE ME A BREAK, CREST, I JUST PLAYED HIDE THE SAUSAGE WITH A BEACHED WHALE.

WE'LL TAKE THE LIFT.

NEXT PROG ▷ TO CATCH A THIEF

HOTEL YALTA, ON THE COAST OF THE BLACK SEA. THE SUITE OF NIKOLAI DANTE.

Nikolai Dante

THE GENTLEMAN THIEF PART 3

Ahh fuoco...

Yiii!

THERE'S YOUR GENTLEMAN THIEF, NIKOLAI DANTE!

OBVIOUSLY I USE THE WORD GENTLEMAN WITH THE LOOSEST POSSIBLE INTERPRETATION.

WHAT'S GOING ON, KONIGSBERG? THE YALTA'S SUPPOSED TO BE NEUTRAL TERRITORY, YET YOU'RE LETTING ARBATOV PURSUE HIS VENDETTA AGAINST ME?

NOT AT ALL, DANTE. I'M MERELY ENFORCING OUR ONLY LAW.

NO ONE HERE GETS OUT ALIVE WITHOUT PAYING THEIR BILL!

SCRIPT
ROBBIE MORRISON

ART
SIMON FRASER

COLOURS
ALISON KIRKPATRICK

LETTERS
ANNIE PARKHOUSE

CAPTAIN ARBATOV HAS FORMULATED A *MOST INTERESTING* THEORY AROUND YOU.

FOR THE LAST MONTH, DANTE, YOU'VE BEEN THROWING THE BIGGEST PARTY IN THE HISTORY OF THE *YALTA*, *SEEMINGLY*, AT THE EXPENSE OF THE ROMANOV DYNASTY.

HOWEVER...

AN EXAMINATION OF ROMANOV STATECRAFT REVEALS THAT THE WEALTH OF THE DYNASTIC ELITE IS DRAWN FROM THE LAND THEY OWN.

WHATEVER THEY SPEND IS *DEDUCTED* FROM THESE FIEFDOMS— NOT NORMALLY A PROBLEM, FOR THEIR HOLDINGS ARE EXTENSIVE.

YOU, HOWEVER, ARE THE GOVERNOR OF *RUDINSHTEIN*, THE *POOREST* CITY IN THE EMPIRE.

I HADN'T EVEN *HEARD* OF IT WHEN I BEGAN MY INVESTIGATION.

YOU'VE *ALREADY* SPENT ENOUGH TO *BANKRUPT* RUDINSHTEIN *SEVERAL* TIMES OVER.

THE ROMANOVS ARE NOT RENOWNED FOR THEIR *TOLERANCE*— A CITY WHICH NO LONGER PROFITED THEM WOULD BE *SEVERELY* PUNISHED.

DANTE HAS OBVIOUSLY RESORTED TO THIEVERY IN AN ATTEMPT TO PAY HIS HOTEL BILL AND SAVE HIS CITY FROM SLAUGHTER OR SLAVERY.

I REST MY CASE.

AND *VERY* ENTERTAINING IT WAS TOO, THOUGH PERSONALLY I'D HAVE SPICED IT UP WITH A LITTLE *SEX* AND *VIOLENCE*.

YOU HAVE MY *THANKS*, CAPTAIN.

YOUR THANKS, THIEF.? I DIDN'T TAKE YOU FOR THE *PENITENT* SORT.

PENITENCE BE *DAMNED*. I'M JUST GLAD YOU GAVE ME THE CHANCE TO DO *THIS*...

AAAGH·KK!

THAT WASN'T AN ADMISSION OF *GUILT*, LORD KONIGSBERG, IT WAS AN EXPRESSION OF *INNOCENCE*.

SUBDUE HIM, ENFORCERS!

The balcony, Dante. It's the easiest escape route...

THE *EASIEST*!?

WE'RE ON THE *110TH* FLOOR!

GGGNNHH!

DON'T JUST STAND THERE, FOOLS... FIRE!!

NICE SHOOTING, BOYS!

KEEP IT UP!

HHHLLKK!

YOU SHOT YOUR OWN MEN, ARBATOV.

NOT TO WORRY. THEY WERE ONLY CONSCRIPTS.

CAPTAIN!

THANKS FOR THE GETAWAY VEHICLE!

WHOA!

THE STEEDS ARE **BIO-LINKED** TO THEIR PILOTS. IT TAKES **HOURS** TO BREAK THE CODE—AND **SECONDS** TO REACH THE GROUND!

I HOPE YOUR CAMERAS CATCH HIS FALL. THE TSAR WILL PAY **HANDSOMELY** TO SEE NIKOLAI DANTE **SPLATTERED** OVER—

NO!

IT'S NOT POSSIBLE!

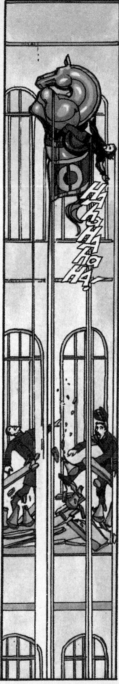

HA HA HA HA

I COULD'VE USED YOU BEFORE I JOINED THE ARISTOCRACY, CREST—**HOTWIRING HARDWARE** WAS NEVER A TALENT OF MINE.

It's not exactly what I was designed for either.

RELAX. ENJOY THE RIDE.

I'VE BEEN RUNNING FROM THE LAW SINCE I WAS OLD ENOUGH TO WALK.

Then it's truly a wonder you ever reached puberty...

BOJEMOI! **GUNHAWKS!**

Get out of the air, Dante, we're too easy a target—the GunHawks outclass us in speed, manoeuvrability and firepower.

OKAY! OKAY OKAY!

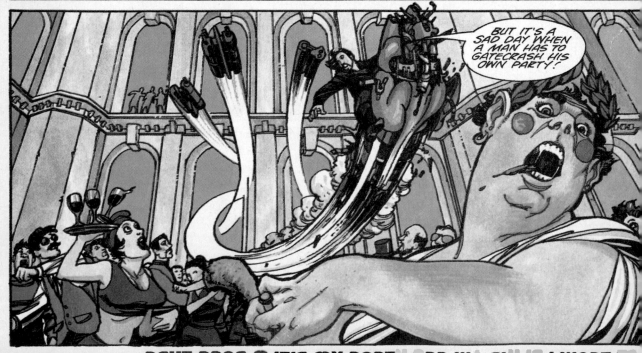

BUT IT'S A SAD DAY WHEN A MAN HAS TO GATECRASH HIS OWN PARTY!

THIS IS AN OUTRAGE, YOU YOUNG ROGUE!

I, GENERAL SHITOV, ORDER YOU TO STOP!

'Accused of thievery by the irate owners of Hotel Yalta, Dante defended his integrity in time-honoured outlaw tradition.

'He ran like hell.' — *BRIGANDS OF THE EMPIRE*, BY MARIA BERIA.

HEY!

IT'S MY PARTY AND I'LL FLY IF I WANT TO!

Nikolai Dante

THE GENTLEMAN THIEF PART 4

WHO INVITED YOU ANYWAY, LARDASS!?

TURGENEV TO LORD KONIGSBERG. DANTE IS IN THE GAMBLING SECTOR.

ORDERS?

HOLD HIM UNTIL CAPTAIN ARBATOV AND I ARRIVE.

BUT DON'T HURT HIM TOO BADLY — THAT'LL BE OUR PLEASURE.

SCRIPT
ROBBIE MORRISON

ART
SIMON FRASER

COLOURS
ALISON KIRKPATRICK

LETTERS
ANNIE PARKHOUSE

Evasive action, Dante. That's a Berez Enforcer blocking our flightpath.

They're recruited from the colony world of Berezova. Planetary conditions there are far harsher than our own.

Due to Earth's lower gravity, the Enforcers' strength and power are incredible.

YEAH!? SO'S OUR SPEED!

And so is your overconfidence...

FUOCO!

YOU'D NEED A TANK TO STOP A BEREZ ENFORCER, THIEF.

THIEF?

DANTE!?

LET'S BRING THE HOUSE DOWN ON HIM, CREST!

STEALING *KISSES* FROM THE *WRONG* PEOPLE AGAIN, NIKOLAI DANTE?

SOMETHING LIKE THAT, *COUNTESSA.*

HEY! WHOA!

YOU *KNEW* IT WAS ME IN YOUR *BEDCHAMBER?*

OF COURSE.

A WOMAN OF *MY* BREEDING CAN TELL A *LOT* FROM A KISS.

DANTE!

YOU'RE NOT DOING TOO WELL, *ENFORCER.*

HERE! TRY YOUR LUCK ON THE ROULETTE WHEEL!

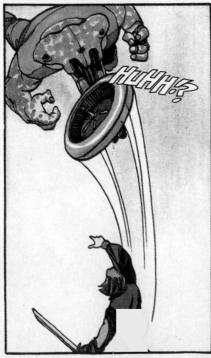

HUHH!?

HHHGGLLPPP!

MY SINCEREST APOLOGIES FOR THIS DISTURBANCE, COUNTESSA DE WINTER. WHERE DID DANTE GO?

THERE. TO THE YALTA'S COMMAND CENTRE.

C'MON. C'MON.

PALMPRINT ACCEPTED. RETINAL SCAN ACCEPTED.

IDENTITY CONFIRMED.

WHY WOULD ANYONE WHO CAN'T PAY THEIR BILL BE LUNATIC ENOUGH TO ENTER THE COMMAND CENTRE?

WHAT KEPT YOU, GENTLEMEN!?

IF YOU WISH TO CHECK, I BELIEVE YOU'LL FIND MY BILL HAS BEEN PAID. IN FULL.

AND I BELIEVE IT'S TIME YOU PAID FOR YOUR CRIMES!

IN FULL!

CAPTAIN, I'M THE ONLY VICTIM OF THE GENTLEMAN THIEF HERE.

I'M THE ONLY ONE WHO CAN PROPERLY IDENTIFY HIM.

HOW!?

I'M AFRAID DANTE'S *NOT* YOUR THIEF—HIS TONGUE IS TOO *SHORT* AND HE *DROOLS* TOO MUCH.

A LADY OF THE COUNTESSA'S BREEDING CAN TELL A *LOT* FROM A KISS.

LORD KONIGSBERG, THE BILL FOR DANTE'S PARTY *HAS* BEEN SETTLED—*BY ORDER OF THE TSAR.* PAYMENT AUTHORISED BY *CAPTAIN ARBATOV.*

IMPOSSIBLE!

DANTE HACKED INTO YOUR SYSTEM!

ISN'T THE *FINANCIAL SECURITY* OF THE YALTA *IMPREGNABLE?*

YOUR GUESTS WOULD SOON DESERT YOU IF THEY THOUGHT THEIR ACCOUNTS COULD FALL VICTIM TO FRAUD OR HACKING.

YEAH, THERE'S NO ONE *TIGHTER* WITH MONEY THAN THE LORDS AND LADIES OF THE THIEVES' WORLD.

UH, OF COURSE OUR *UH,* SECURITY IS IMPREGNABLE.

ENFORCERS, SUBDUE ARBATOV—THE TSAR WON'T BE PLEASED TO LEARN HOW YOU'VE *SQUANDERED* HIS REGIMENT'S MONEY, CAPTAIN.

DAMN YOU, DANTE— **GGLLRRKK!**

THIS PARTY'S *OVER,* COUNTESSA.

MAYBE WE SHOULD GO TO MY SUITE AND START ONE OF OUR—

'COUNTESSA?'

A Weapons Crest is an instrument of honour and nobility. You used me to forge Arbatov's palm and retina prints, then defraud the Yalta of the money you rightfully owed them.

HONOUR BE DAMNED, CREST.

WE HAD SOME *FUN*, SAVED RUDINSHTEIN, *PAID* MY HOTEL BILL AND *EVEN* MANAGED TO KEEP THE GENTLEMAN THIEF'S SPOILS.

THE ONLY THING I *LOST* WAS THE COUNTESSA DE WINTER.

WHAT THE HELL...

WE'VE GOT A SMALL FORTUNE HERE. LET'S CONSOLE OURSELVES BY *ROLLING* AROUND IN —

A PAIR OF KNICKERS!? WHERE'S MY MONEY!?

Judging from the message on her underwear, the Countessa's kisses may have concealed an ulterior motive...

DAMN! AND I THOUGHT SHE WAS AFTER MY BODY...

FOR EVERY GENTLEMAN THIEF, THERE'S A LADY WHO'LL STEAL HIS HEART

THE END

THE FULL DANTE

Script: Robbie Morrison

Art: Charlie Adlard

Letters: Annie Parkhouse

Originally published in *2000 AD* Prog 1071

Nikolai Dante

NEVER GET INVOLVED WITH MORE THAN THREE WOMEN AT ONE TIME, KOLYA.

I ONCE TRIED TO ENTERTAIN SEVEN SEDUCTRESSES IN A MIRRORED ZERO-GRAVITY CHAMBER.

AFTER AN EMBARRASSINGLY SHORT TIME, THEY BEGAN ENTERTAINING THEMSELVES. IT LOWERED MY SPIRITS SOMEWHAT.

KOLYA?

THE QUIVERING FLESHPOT

'The Cossacks! Stallions Of The Steppes!' The sexiest dance troupe to ever strut their sculptured waves before the noblewomen of the Empire!
— ONE OF THE MORE MODEST TURNS OF PHRASE FROM THE COSSACKS' TOUR PROGRAMME.

GET 'EM OUT FOR THE LADIES!

GET 'EM OFF!

LADIES! LADIES! LADIES!

WHY WORK YOURSELVES INTO A LATHER OVER THESE —HIC!— PREENING, PUMPED-UP POSEURS WHEN YOU'VE GOT A PRIME SPECIMEN OF THE IMPERIAL ARISTOCRACY IN YOUR MIDST?

YOU!? YOU'RE EVERYTHING THAT'S WRONG WITH THE ARISTOCRACY— AN ARROGANT, INBRED, VODKA-SWILLING, CIGAR-PUFFING SLOB!

OUR BODIES ARE *TEMPLES*, WORKS OF ART. *VANITY* PLAYS NO PART IN OUR APPEARANCE!

But if you don't stop hogging our limelight, we'll kill you.

I'M TOO— hic!— COOL TO KILL...

PUT *THAT* IN YOUR POUCH AND SMOKE IT!

LADIES! THE NAME'S *NANTE* —hic!— *DIKOLAI NANTE*. IF YOU WANT TO TEST THE FIRMNESS OF RUSSIAN *MANHOOD*, FEEL FREE TO *FONDLE* MINE.

OOFFF!

Dante, in your present state of inebriation, your crude, dirty-fighting techniques may prove less than effective.

EVEN *TOTALLY SMASHED*, CREST...

THERE'S NO WAY I'M GETTING MY HEAD POUNDED IN BY A *POSSE* OF *POSING POUCHES!*

AHHHH!

AOWW! MY MOUSTACHE! AOWW!

AOWWWWWW!

KROUFF!

AFTER THAT, WHAT COULD I POSSIBLY DO FOR AN ENCORE?

GET 'EM OFF AND GET 'EM OUT!

WE PAID TO MAKE FUN OF SOME *DANGLY BITS*, AND BY *VLADIMIR'S BEARD*, WE BETTER SEE THEM!

DIAVOLO!

IF THERE'S ONE THING MORE DANGEROUS THAN A WOMAN SCORNED, IT'S A WHOLE ARMY OF THEM SCORNED. BUT IF YOU CAN'T BEAT THEM...

LIGHTS...
MUSIC...
ACTION!

I'm beginning to get the impression that you're enjoying this sordid show a little more than you should be, Dante...

SPLUTCH!

Tut, tut, tut...

NO SELF-CONTROL— THAT'S THE TROUBLE WITH AMATEURS.

DON'T ALL *FAINT* AT ONCE, LADIES...

THE FULL DANTE'S STILL TO COME!

THWUMPH!

I believe you require a longer shaft to properly execute the pole vault, Dante.

Tell me...

Does losing your clothes and being forced to return home in a pair of animal-pube underpants normally constitute a quiet evening out? Another man's pants at that...

I'M *TELLING* YOU, CREST, IF YOU WEREN'T *BONDED* TO ME...

THE END

MOSCOW DUELLISTS

Script: Robbie Morrison

Art: Simon Fraser

Colors: Alison Kirkpatrick

Letters: Annie Parkhouse

Originally published in *2000 AD* Progs 1072-1075

THE YEAR OF THE TSAR 2666.
THE IMPERIAL PALACE OF
TSAR VLADIMIR THE CONQUEROR.

IT'S TRULY A *PLEASURE* TO HAVE THE IMPERIAL DYNASTIES AS OUR GUESTS ONCE MORE, ISN'T IT, JENA?

Nikolai Dante

MOSCOW DUELLISTS — PART 1

YES, FATHER, *ESPECIALLY* THE HOUSE OF *ROMANOV.*

SCRIPT
ROBBIE MORRISON
ART
SIMON FRASER
COLOURS
ALISON KIRKPATRICK
LETTERS
ANNIE PARKHOUSE

THIS HISTORIC GATHERING IS TO MARK THE UNVEILING OF A *MONUMENT* TO ALL THE *GLORIES* OF THE EMPIRE AND TO THE *UNQUESTIONED* AUTHORITY OF *MY* RULE.

LOOKING GOOD, JENA!

AND YOU'RE LOOKING LIKE SOMETHING I'D HAVE THE SERVANTS CLEAN OFF MY SHOE, THIEF.

SUCH A MONUMENT OF SUCH *EPIC* SPECTACLE THAT I HAVE HAD ITS ARCHITECTS *BLINDED,* SO THAT THEY MAY NEVER AGAIN CREATE SUCH *BEAUTY.*

PLEASE DON'T THINK MY TREATMENT OF THEM HARSH OR UNKIND.

THEY SHALL REMAIN IN IMPERIAL CARE, PLEASURED FOR LIFE BY THE *MOST BEAUTIFUL SEDUCTRESSES* IN MY EMPLOY.

WE'RE COMING INTO POSITION NOW, TSAR VLADIMIR.

LOCK THE PALACE IN STATIONARY ORBIT, *PYRE,* AND OPEN THE OBSERVATION BAY.

135

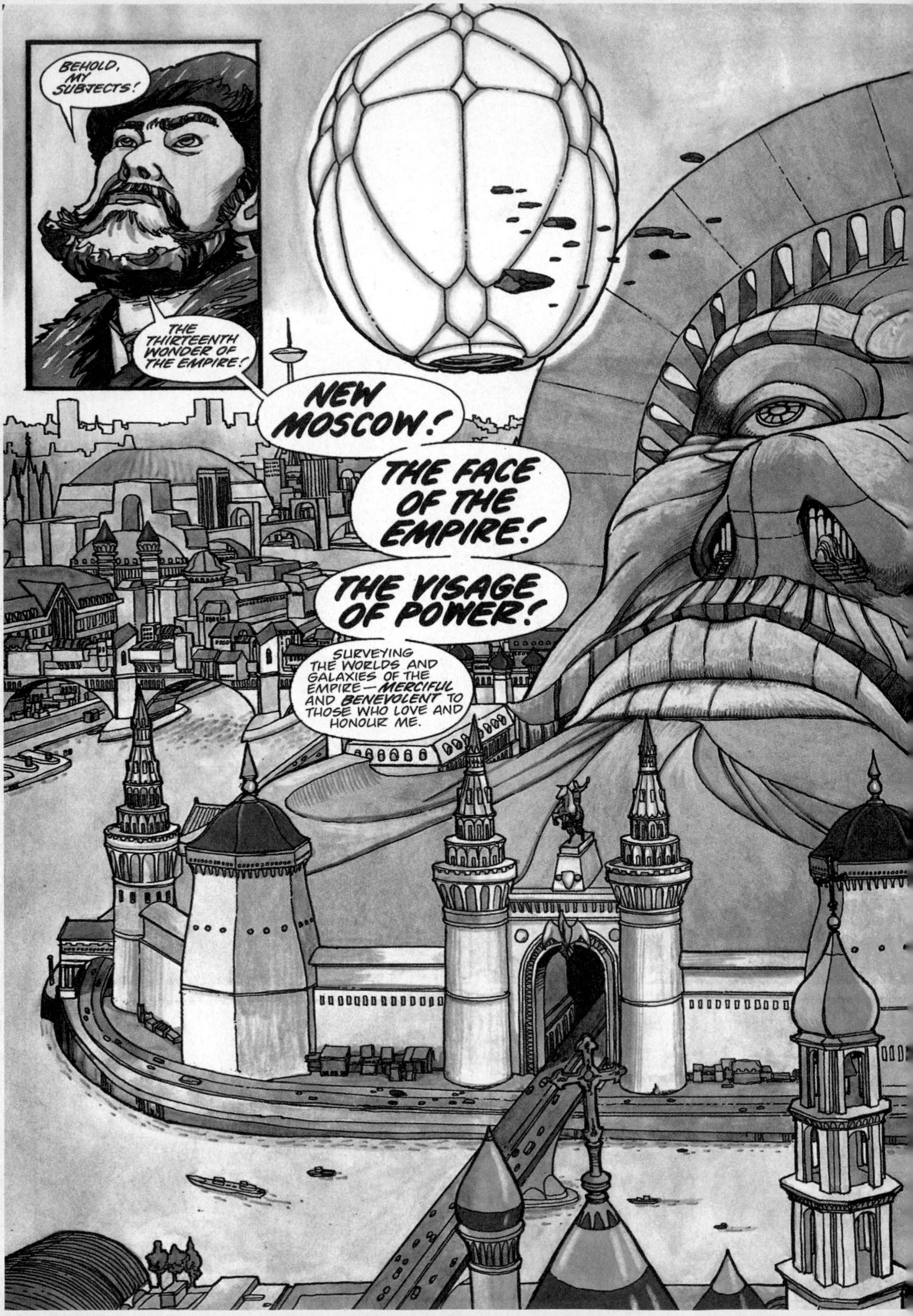
BEHOLD, MY SUBJECTS!
THE THIRTEENTH WONDER OF THE EMPIRE!
NEW MOSCOW!
THE FACE OF THE EMPIRE!
THE VISAGE OF POWER!
SURVEYING THE WORLDS AND GALAXIES OF THE EMPIRE—MERCIFUL AND BENEVOLENT TO THOSE WHO LOVE AND HONOUR ME.

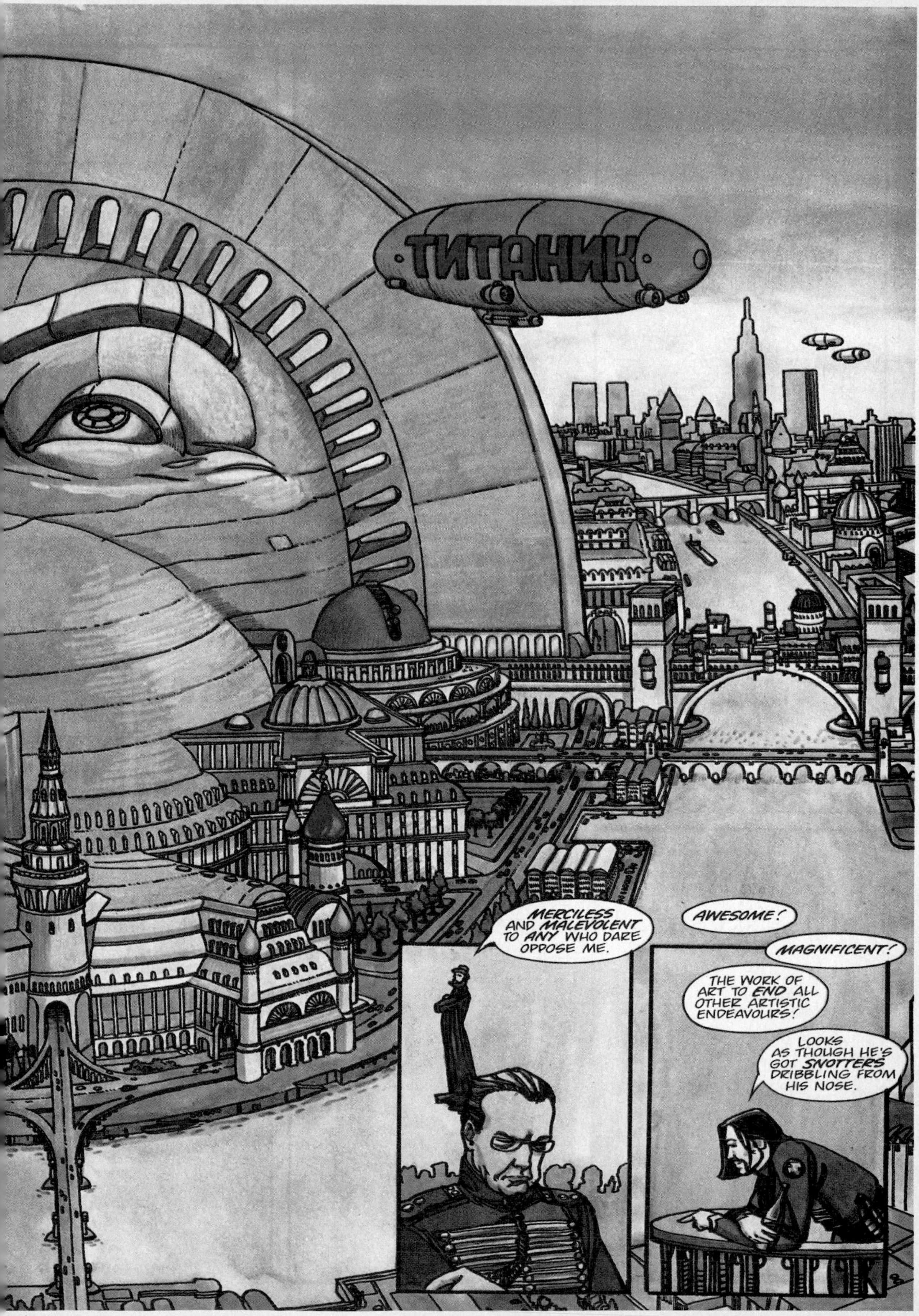
ТИТАНИК
MERCILESS AND MALEVOLENT TO ANY WHO DARE OPPOSE ME.
AWESOME!
MAGNIFICENT!
THE WORK OF ART TO END ALL OTHER ARTISTIC ENDEAVOURS!
LOOKS AS THOUGH HE'S GOT SNOTTERS DRIBBLING FROM HIS NOSE.

THIS IS AN *OUTRAGE*, VLADIMIR!

YOU *RAISED* THE TRIBUTE YOU DEMAND FROM THE DYNASTIES TO BUILD THIS *EGOMANIACAL MONSTROSITY!?*

SUCH *SYMBOLS* OF POWER—*ICONS*, IF YOU WILL—ARE IMPORTANT FOR THE *MORALE* OF MY SUBJECTS.

RULING AN EMPIRE IS NO *CASUAL* AFFAIR, *DMITRI.* *YOU* OF ALL PEOPLE SHOULD KNOW THAT.

THE FAMILY ROMANOV *LOST* THE FIRST EMPIRE AND PLUNGED US INTO *CENTURIES OF CHAOS.*

SURELY AN INCREASE IN TRIBUTE IS A SMALL PRICE TO PAY FOR KEEPING THE PRESENT EMPIRE SAFE IN *MY* CAPABLE HANDS.

Ahh, THE OSTENTATIOUS GRANDEUR OF ARISTOCRATIC LIFE. YOU MUST FIND IT ALL RATHER OVERWHELMING, *LITTLE BROTHER.*

STRAIT·LACED AND BORE·THE·PANTS·OFF· YOU·DULL, KONSTANTIN. BRING ON THE *BEER* AND THE *DANCING GIRLS...*

LET'S *MINGLE*, NIKOLAI. I'LL FAMILIARISE YOU WITH SOME OF THE OTHER GUESTS—I *KNOW* EVERYONE.

YOU GET AROUND THEN, *NASTASIA?*

THE HOUSE OF *RASPUTIN*, A.K.A. THE *DEVIL'S MARTYRS*. A FANATICUL CULT DEVOTED TO OUR FAMILY'S OLD NEMESIS *GRIGORI RASPUTIN.*

THE HIGHER RANKS REPUTEDLY POSSESS PSIONIC POWERS.

I'VE *BRUSHED BRISTLES* WITH THEM BEFORE...

'MIKHAIL DERIABIN, ELECTED HEAD OF THE HOUSE OF BOLSHOI, THE LARGEST MEDIA AND ARTS CONGLOMERATE IN THE EMPIRE...'

'AND HIS LOVER, THE FIREBIRD, BALLERINA QUEEN OF THE DANSE MACABRE.'

'THE BLACK DRAGONS, GOVERNORS OF THE DARK OCEAN AND THE MANY THOUSANDS OF ISLAND COMMUNITIES WITHIN IT.'

'A TREACHEROUS ALLIANCE OF YAKUZA SOCIETIES, CURRENTLY CHAIRED, SOMEWHAT MURDEROUSLY, BY THE SAGAWA CLAN.'

'REPRESENTATIVES FROM THE HOUSES OF NUMA, TANTOR AND KONG, CONTROLLERS OF THE FORMER AFRICAN CONTINENT.'

'EVOLVED FROM ENDANGERED SPECIES SEEDED WITH HUMAN INTELLIGENCE TO PROMOTE THEIR SURVIVAL, THEY WIPED OUT THEIR HUMAN AGGRESSORS AND ASSUMED POWER.'

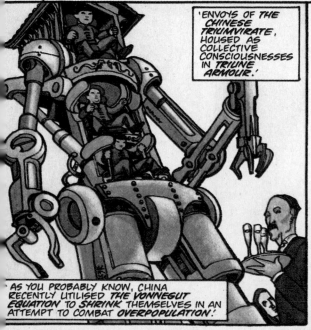

'ENVOYS OF THE CHINESE TRIUMVIRATE, HOUSED AS COLLECTIVE CONSCIOUSNESSES IN TRIUNE ARMOUR.'

AS YOU PROBABLY KNOW, CHINA RECENTLY UTILISED THE VONNEGUT EQUATION TO SHRINK THEMSELVES IN AN ATTEMPT TO COMBAT OVERPOPULATION.'

CAIUS ZACHAROVITCH, THE FENCING MASTER.

HE WAS GIVEN CONTROL OF THE KARAZIN'S LANDS WHEN THE TSAR OUTLAWED THEM.

WE WERE FORCED TO USE YOUR TRIBUTE FOR THE TREATMENT OF CASUALTIES AND THE RECONSTRUCTION OF THE CITY FOLLOWING THE TIKUNOV EARTHQUATE.

ALL I HAVE TO OFFER YOU, TSAR VLADIMIR, IS MY SWORD.

YOUR SWORD, YOUR LOYALTY AND YOUR FRIENDSHIP ARE MORE THAN TRIBUTE ENOUGH FOR US, CAIUS.

JENA, MY LOVE. DO NOT THINK, BECAUSE YOU ARE MY DAUGHTER, THAT YOU MAY SPEAK FOR ME.

EVER.

KOLYA, THESE GATHERINGS ARE DANGEROUS—THERE'S A LOT OF HOSTILITY BETWEEN THE DYNASTIES.

WE ROMANOVS ARE USUALLY SAFE FROM ATTACK, BUT YOU MIGHT BE SEEN AS AN EASY TARGET.

ANDREAS...

I'M EASY, BUT NOT THAT EASY.

I'LL WAGER YOUNG NIKOLAI'S DEAD, DYING, MAIMED OR WOUNDED IN LESS THAN TEN MINUTES.

DO I HAVE A BET?

I WISH YOU'D STOP TEMPTING ME, LULU—YOU KNOW I CAN'T RESIST INDULGING IN VICES.

THINGS ARE LOOKING UP, EH, SVENGIS?

NOT QUITE THE PHRASE I'D USE SLOBODAN...

NEXT PROG ▷ THE DANGER OF DIRTY THOUGHTS

'The breathtaking unveiling of New Moscow was somewhat overshadowed by the celebrations that followed.

'In particular, the audacious behaviour of a man fast becoming a permanent fixture in the scandal pages of this publication...

Nikolai Dante

MOSCOW DUELLISTS PART 2

"...Nikolai Dante, illegitimate sibling of the Romanov Dynasty!'— THE IMPERIAL TIMES.

Assassinations and duels are de rigueur amongst the noble Houses at these events. Give no one an excuse to challenge you.

If you're a gentleman, then chivalry has finally curled up and died.

SCRIPT
ROBBIE MORRISON

ART
SIMON FRASER

COLOURS
ALISON KIRKPATRICK

LETTERS
ANNIE PARKHOUSE

RELAX, CREST, I'LL BE THE *EPITOME* OF AN *IMPERIAL GENTLEMAN*.

THAT WAS MY WIFE, YOU DOG!

NEVER IN A LIFETIME OF *DEPRAVITY* HAVE I EXPERIENCED SUCH *OFFENSIVE THOUGHTS!*

I DEMAND *SATISFACTION* THROUGH *TRIAL BY COMBAT!* NAME THE TIME!

UH, TOMORROW?

AFTER MY HANGOVER'S CLEARED?

AGREED. MY MEN WILL CONTACT YOU.

Elders of the House of Rasputin possess psychic powers. Obviously he probed your 'gentlemanly' thoughts towards his wife.

WHAT'S THE WORLD COMING TO WHEN A MAN CAN'T EVEN *THINK* IN PEACE?

I DIDN'T KNOW YOU HAD *INTELLECTUAL* LEANINGS, NIKOLAI. I PRESUMED YOUR MIND WAS *BLISSFULLY* FREE OF *ALL* THOUGHT.

NOT *ALL* THOUGHT, JENA.

THE *DIRTY* ONES ARE AIMED STRAIGHT AT *YOU*...

YOU FILTHY, ARROGANT, SEWER-BRED RAT!

LANGUAGE LIKE THAT COULD ONLY COME FROM A MIND AT *LEAST* AS DIRTY AS MINE...

'COURSE, THEY DO SAY GREAT MINDS THINK ALIKE.

AND I THINK THEY SHOULD *COME* TOGETHER TOO... FOR *PASSIONATE* DEBATE.

Y'KNOW, YOU'LL PUT SOMEONE'S *EYE* OUT WITH *THAT*.

WHY, MILADY, WHAT *ARE* YOU TALKING ABOUT?

YOUR SWORD, THIEF...

AAOOWW

THERE, THERE, YOU'LL BE ALRIGHT.

DO YOU WANT PRINCESS JENA TO KISS IT BETTER?

CLUMSY BARBARIAN! I AM NOT A *CHILD!*

THE ROMANOV PIG HAS BLINDED NUMBER 336!

HEY! WHOA!

IT WAS AN ACCIDENT!

CRUSH HIS LOFTY ARROGANCE!

CUT HIM DOWN TO SIZE!

HHAA!!

KKKYEEH!

THERE'S NO WAY I'M GETTING DONE IN BY THE SEVEN DWARVES!

WWAAAHHH!

STRIKE ONE FOR THE MAN IN ROMANOV RED.

TIME FOR ANOTHER DRINK, I THINK...

HEY, VIKTOR.

HOW'S IT GOING?

THAT, SIRRR, WAS THE *LAST* BANANA! AND IT HAD *MY* NAME ON IT!

HUH!?

HAS THE WHOLE WORLD GONE *MAD* OR SOMETHING!?

I'M BEING HASSLED ABOUT A *BANANA* BY A *TALKING APE!?*

BANANAS ARE OF *GRRREAT* IMPORRRTANCE TO THE HOUSE OF *KONG.*

I DEMAND SATISFACTION THRRROUGH--

TRIAL BY COMBAT!? *UH UH!* YOU WANT A FIGHT, *FUZZY*, LET'S GO FOR IT! HERE AND NOW, YOU AND ME!

WHO DARES?

WHOA!

HALT! THERE SHALL BE **NO BLOODSHED** IN THE IMPERIAL PALACE. ALL DISPUTES WILL BE SETTLED THROUGH **OFFICIALLY-SANCTIONED** DUELS.

I'LL GLADLY *RRRIP* HIM LIMB FROM LIMB IN *YOURRR* NAME, TSARRR VLADIMIRRR.

DANTE ALREADY HAS A PRIOR ENGAGEMENT— WITH *ME.*

HE PLAYED **PINBALL** WITH THE ENVOYS OF THE CHINESE TRIUMVIRATE! WE DEMAND SATISFACTION THROUGH *TRIAL BY COMBAT!*

Bojemoi... it never rains but it pours...

EXCELLENT!

THE DUELS SHALL FORM A *TOURNAMENT,* THE *BLOOD* OF WHICH WILL *CHRISTEN* MY NEW CITY.

OF COURSE, YOUNG DANTE...

WHILE I'M *GRATEFUL* FOR THE *ENTERTAINMENT OPPORTUNITY* YOU'VE CREATED, I CAN *HARDLY* IGNORE THE *DISHONOURABLE WAY* IN WHICH YOU'VE REPAID MY HOSPITALITY.

CAIUS ZACHAROVITCH. YOU SHALL FIGHT DANTE ON BEHALF OF MYSELF AND THE EMPIRE.

THE BOY HASN'T INSULTED *ME,* SIRE. THE RULES OF DUELLING STATE THAT *PERSONAL HONOUR*--

HE HAS INSULTED *ME,* CAIUS. AND AS YOU SAID, *YOUR SWORD IS MINE.* I HOPE YOU INTEND TO *HONOUR* YOUR WORD.

YES, TSAR VLADIMIR.

145

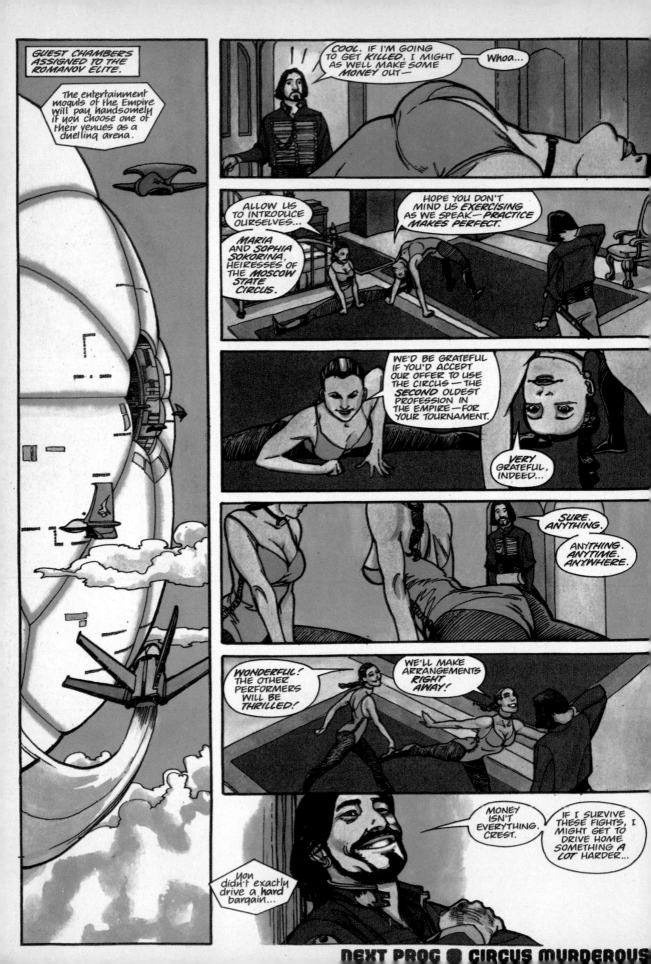

GUEST CHAMBERS ASSIGNED TO THE ROMANOV ELITE.

The entertainment moguls of the Empire will pay handsomely if you choose one of their venues as a duelling arena.

COOL. IF I'M GOING TO GET *KILLED*, I MIGHT AS WELL MAKE SOME *MONEY* OUT—

Whoa...

ALLOW US TO INTRODUCE OURSELVES... MARIA AND *SOPHIA SOKORINA*, HEIRESSES OF THE *MOSCOW STATE CIRCUS*.

HOPE YOU DON'T MIND US *EXERCISING* AS WE SPEAK—*PRACTICE MAKES PERFECT*.

WE'D BE GRATEFUL IF YOU'D ACCEPT OUR OFFER TO USE THE CIRCUS—THE *SECOND OLDEST PROFESSION IN THE EMPIRE*—FOR YOUR TOURNAMENT.

VERY GRATEFUL, INDEED...

SURE. ANYTHING.

ANYTHING. ANYTIME. ANYWHERE.

WONDERFUL! THE OTHER PERFORMERS WILL BE *THRILLED!*

WE'LL MAKE ARRANGEMENTS *RIGHT AWAY!*

MONEY ISN'T EVERYTHING, CREST.

IF I SURVIVE THESE FIGHTS, I MIGHT GET TO DRIVE HOME SOMETHING A *LOT* HARDER...

You didn't exactly drive a hard bargain...

NEXT PROG ● CIRCUS MURDEROUS

Dante

NEW MOSCOW IMPERIAL CIRCUS.

MOSCOW DUELLISTS PART 3

Nikolai Dante

ALFREDO MARCONI & HIS ACROBATIC **ELEPHANTS**

The Flying STRONZI

'Often, he who was in the right nevertheless lost the battle.' — HONORÉ BONET, 1387, REFLECTING ON THE RIDICULOUSNESS AND FUTILITY OF DUELS TO THE DEATH.

QUITE A *CROWD*.

I'M ALWAYS A BIG DRAW—*ESPECIALLY* WHEN THERE'S A GOOD CHANCE I MIGHT GET MYSELF *KILLED*.

AND WHAT ARE YOU HERE FOR, *JENA*?

COME TO GRANT A *HORNY* CONDEMNED MAN HIS *LAST* REQUEST?

SCRIPT
ROBBIE MORRISON
ART
SIMON FRASER
COLOURS
ALISON KIRKPATRICK
LETTERS
ANNIE PARKHOUSE

AU CONTRAIRE, NIKOLAI, I'VE COME TO *GLOAT*. WHEN *CAIUS ZACHAROVITCH* KILLS YOU TONIGHT, I'LL BE THE ONE YOU HEAR *CHEERING LOUDEST*.

HE'S A *HERO*, THE MOST *FAMOUS* DUELLIST IN THE EMPIRE.

HE WAS MY *FENCING TUTOR* FOR YEARS, ALMOST LIKE A *FATHER* TO ME. HE TAUGHT ME EVERYTHING I KNOW.

AND REMEMBER WHAT HAPPENED WHEN *WE* CROSSED BLADES?

YEAH, WE ENDED UP WITH OUR *TONGUES* DOWN EACH OTHER'S *THROATS*...

AND IT'S *WAY* PAST TIME FOR A *REMATCH*.

GGGNNNPH

Y'KNOW, *CREST*, I THINK SHE'S FINALLY BEGINNING TO *FALL* FOR ME.

And how do you arrive at that conclusion?

She just burst your nose across your face...

YEAH, BUT SHE HAD A *SWORD* IN HER HAND — SHE COULD'VE *SLIT* MY *THROAT*.

MILORDS AND LADIES!

THE IMPERIAL CIRCUS IS PLEASED TO BRING YOU A DUELLING TOURNAMENT TO CELEBRATE THE OPENING OF NEW MOSCOW AND THE RULE OF VLADIMIR THE CONQUEROR!

NIKOLAI DANTE, ACCUSED OF ALMOST EVERY INSULT UNDER THE SUN, WILL DEFEND HIS HONOUR AGAINST FOUR ASSAILANTS...

INQUISITOR KLYASKA OF THE DEVIL'S MARTYRS, NUMBERS 333, 336 AND 369 OF THE CHINESE TRIUMVIRATE.

GENERAL LIRKO OF THE HOUSE OF KONG AND CAIUS ZACHAROVITCH, THE FENCING MASTER!

COMBATANTS-- ENTER THE ARENA AND DO YOUR DUTY!

UH, THE DUEL STARTS AS SOON AS WE STEP INTO THE RING?

OF COURSE, BOY! DIDN'T YOU EVEN FAMILIARISE YOURSELF WITH THE RULES?

UUURRKK!

DIDN'T READ MY MIND THAT TIME, DID YOU?

NEXT!

HHHLLGG!

YOU DON'T *DESERVE* THE *HONOUR* OF *FAIR COMBAT,* ROMANOV!

WE'LL *WHIP* YOU LIKE THE *TREACHEROUS DOG* YOU ARE!

Weapons analysis: Triune Armour, which coalesces its weavers' minds into a collective consciousness.

D'AVOLO!

NO, YOU *STUNTED* FOOLS... YOU'VE THROWN HIM *BACKSTAGE!*

WHOA...

TALK ABOUT *SKIDMARKS!*

SLICE HIM IN *THREE!*

WE'LL BE *PROMOTED* FOR THIS!

NO *LONGER* SHALL WE *SKULK* IN THE *LOW HUNDREDS* AS 333, 336 AND 359...

THWA-K!

WE'LL *STAND TALL* IN THE *THOUSANDS* AS 999, 1008 AND—

WHAT...!?

KERRUMP!

151

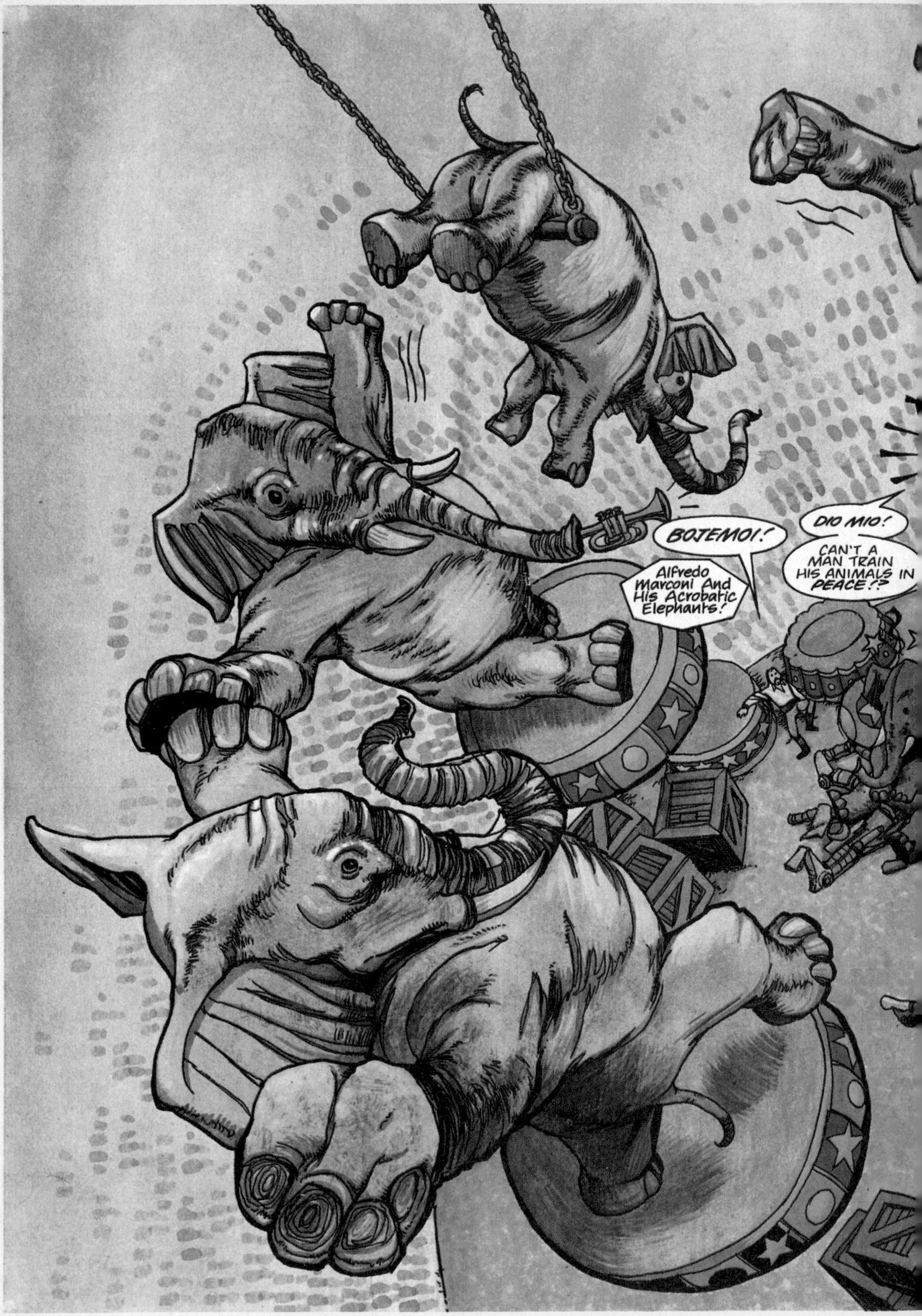
BOJEMOI!
Alfredo Marconi And His Acrobatic Elephants!
DIO MIO!
CAN'T A MAN TRAIN HIS ANIMALS IN PEACE!?

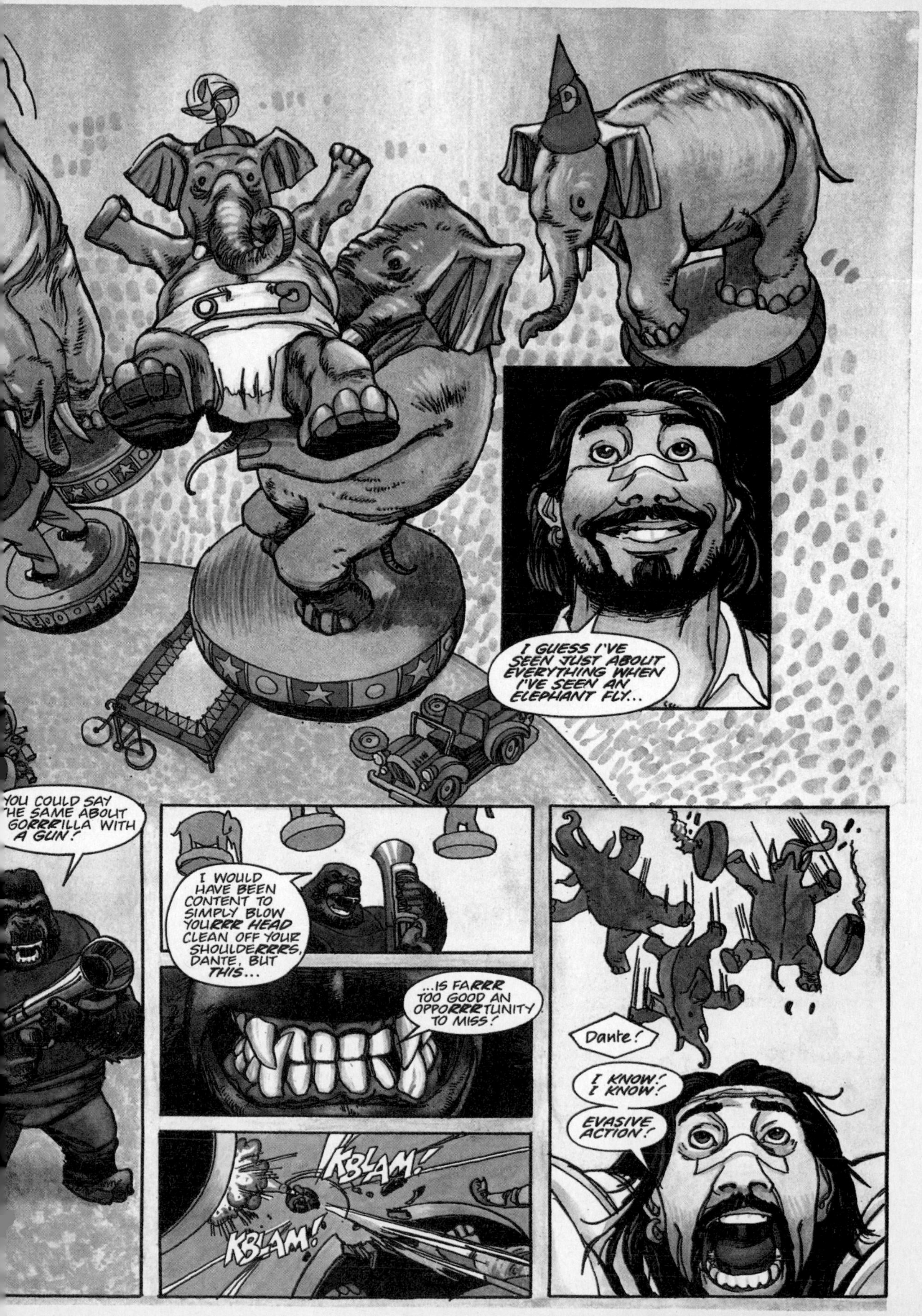

I GUESS I'VE SEEN JUST ABOUT EVERYTHING WHEN I'VE SEEN AN ELEPHANT FLY...
YOU COULD SAY THE SAME ABOUT GORRRILLA WITH A GUN!
I WOULD HAVE BEEN CONTENT TO SIMPLY BLOW YOURRR HEAD CLEAN OFF YOUR SHOULDERRRS, DANTE, BUT THIS...
...IS FARRR TOO GOOD AN OPPORRRTUNITY TO MISS!
KBLAM!
KBLAM!
Dante!
I KNOW! I KNOW!
EVASIVE ACTION!

NEXT PROG FIRST BLOOD!

'The noble tradition of duelling reached its nadir during the infamous New Moscow tournament, when Nikolai Dante was challenged by warriors from four noble houses!'

Nikolai Dante

MOSCOW DUELLISTS PART 4

SCRIPT ROBBIE MORRISON
ART SIMON FRASER
COLOURS ALISON KIRKPATRICK
LETTERS ANNIE PARKHOUSE

'Choice of weapons was elephantine, to say the least...' — A HISTORY OF DUELLING, IVAN GERASSIM.

HA HA HAHA!

NEW MOSCOW IMPERIAL CIRCUS.

THIS IS FARCICAL.

MY SUBJECTS PAID TO CHEER THE DEATH OF NIKOLAI DANTE, NOT TO YELL ABUSE AT AN EMPTY RING.

UNGAWA!

OOOH! OOOH! OOOH!

DAMN YOU, THIEF!

DAMN YOU!

CAUSS! CAUSS!

LISTEN TO THEM.

THE ARISTOCRACY THE IMPERIAL NOBILITY...

SCREAMING FOR BLOOD, CHEERING ON THEIR *PET KILLERS.*

WHAT? WASN'T IT *ALWAYS* LIKE THIS?

MAYBE.

MAYBE I JUST NEVER *REALISED...*

I PLEDGE TO CONDUCT MYSELF WITH *HONOUR* AND DUEL TO *FIRST BLOOD* IN THE NAME OF TSAR VLADIMIR THE CONQUEROR.

I'LL DEFEND MYSELF WITH *PASSION* AND *PANACHE* AND PROVE WHAT THE *LADIES* OF THE *THIEVES' WORLD* ALREADY *KNOW* — THAT I REALLY AM *TOO COOL TO KILL.*

'COURSE, IF I DON'T, I HOPE YOU'LL ACCEPT A *SHALLOW CUT* ON THE *PINKIE* AS EVIDENCE OF *FIRST BLOOD...*

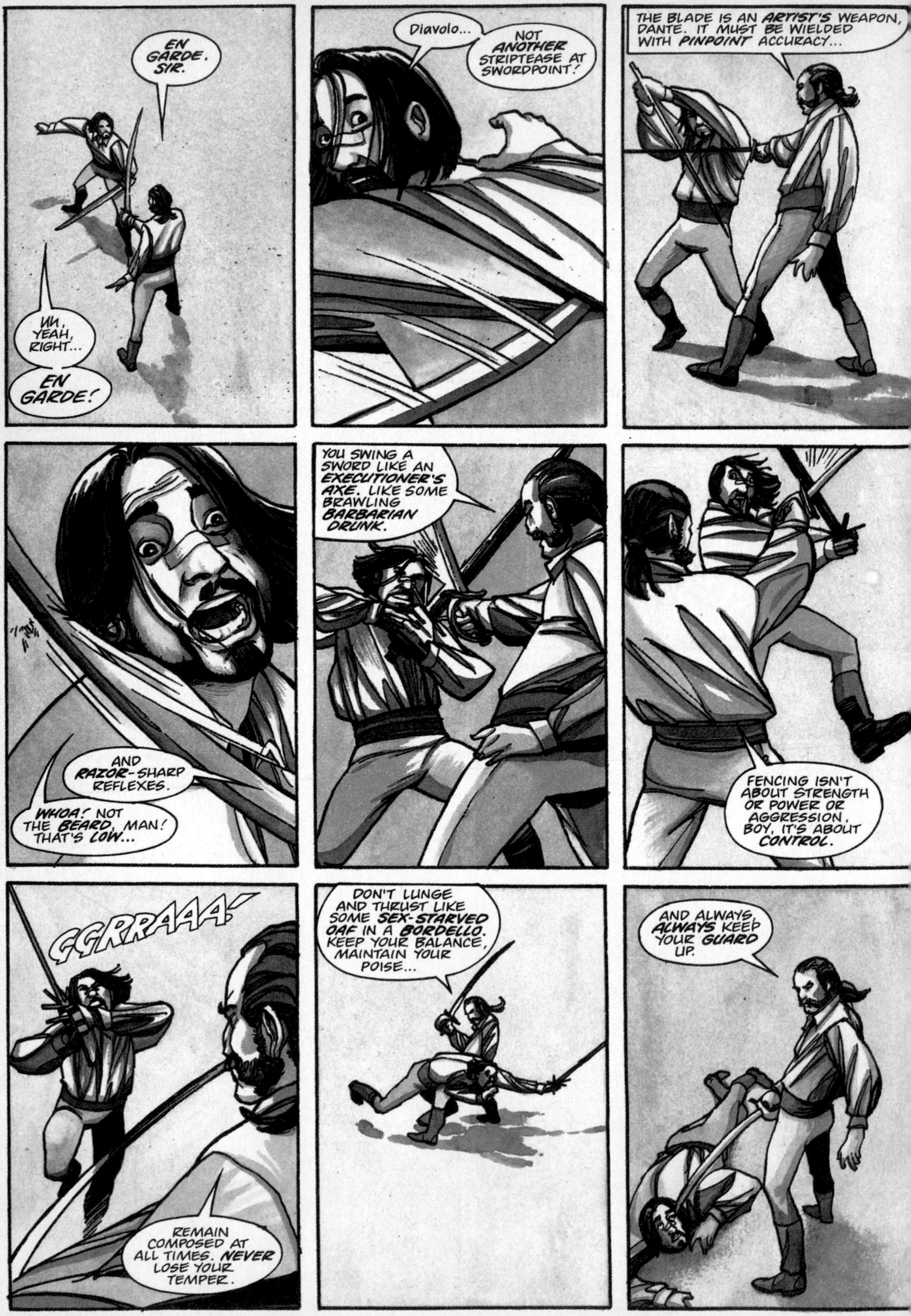

EN GARDE. SIR.
UH, YEAH, RIGHT...
EN GARDE!
Diavolo...
NOT ANOTHER STRIPTEASE AT SWORDPOINT!
THE BLADE IS AN ARTIST'S WEAPON, DANTE. IT MUST BE WIELDED WITH PINPOINT ACCURACY...
AND RAZOR-SHARP REFLEXES.
WHOA! NOT THE BEARD, MAN! THAT'S LOW...
YOU SWING A SWORD LIKE AN EXECUTIONER'S AXE. LIKE SOME BRAWLING BARBARIAN DRUNK.
FENCING ISN'T ABOUT STRENGTH OR POWER OR AGGRESSION, BOY, IT'S ABOUT CONTROL.
GGRRAAA!
REMAIN COMPOSED AT ALL TIMES. NEVER LOSE YOUR TEMPER.
DON'T LUNGE AND THRUST LIKE SOME SEX-STARVED OAF IN A BORDELLO. KEEP YOUR BALANCE, MAINTAIN YOUR POISE...
AND ALWAYS, ALWAYS KEEP YOUR GUARD UP.

FUOCO...

GO ON. DO IT.

FIRST BLOOD, VLADIMIR, THE BOY'S DEFEATED—AND *HUMILIATED*. UNDER THE TRADITIONAL LAWS OF DUELLING, YOUR HONOUR IS *AVENGED*.

I'LL DECIDE THAT, CAIUS.

KILL HIM.

I'VE KILLED *ENOUGH* FOR YOU, VLADIMIR, AND I'M BEGINNING TO DOUBT THAT YOU AND YOUR EMPIRE ARE *WORTH* KILLING FOR.

MAYBE THEY *NEVER WERE*, MAYBE I WAS JUST A *FOOL*...

THEN I HOPE YOUR NEW-FOUND PRINCIPLES ARE WORTH *DYING* FOR, CAIUS.

PYRE!

CAIUS!

JENA, MY LOVE. *COMPOSE* YOURSELF.

NOW.

CAIUS... JENA TOLD ME YOU WERE LIKE A *FATHER* TO HER. THE EMPIRE WOULD BE A BETTER PLACE IF YOU *HAD* BEEN.

KEEP YOUR GUARD UP...

...boy...

'I have no words. My voice is in my sword...' — *SHAKESPEARE, MACBETH.*

THE IMPERIAL PALACE.

DANTE!

Nikolai...

GUEST CHAMBERS ASSIGNED TO THE ROMANOV ELITE.

JENA! WHAT'RE YOU DOING HERE?

I...THIS ISN'T EASY FOR ME TO SAY...

I CAME TO THANK YOU FOR WHAT YOU SAID TO CAIUS IN THE ARENA. IT... WAS *NICE*...

PROBABLY THE MOST *DECENT* THING YOU'VE--

HEH he HEH!

Uh, JENA...

YOU'VE MET *MARIA* AND *SOPHIA SOKORINA?* HEIRESSES TO THE IMPERIAL CIRCUS...

JENA!

Ahh, fuoco...

HEIRESSES IN YOUR BED AND PRINCESSES AT YOUR DOOR...

WHAT KIND OF MAN ARE YOU, NIKOLAI DANTE?

EITHER THE LUCKIEST ONE ALIVE OR THE UNLUCKIEST.

WHAT THE HELL...

AS YOU SAY IN THE CIRCUS, THE SHOW MUST GO ON!

GET READY FOR SOME LOVING!

I'M COMING IN LIKE FLYNN!

COME BACK HERE YOU UNGRATEFUL BEASTS!

THE END

Dante

THE GULAG APOCALYPTIC

Script: Robbie Morrison

Art: Henry Flint

Letters: Annie Parkhouse

Originally published in *2000 AD* Progs 1079-1082

Nikolai Dante

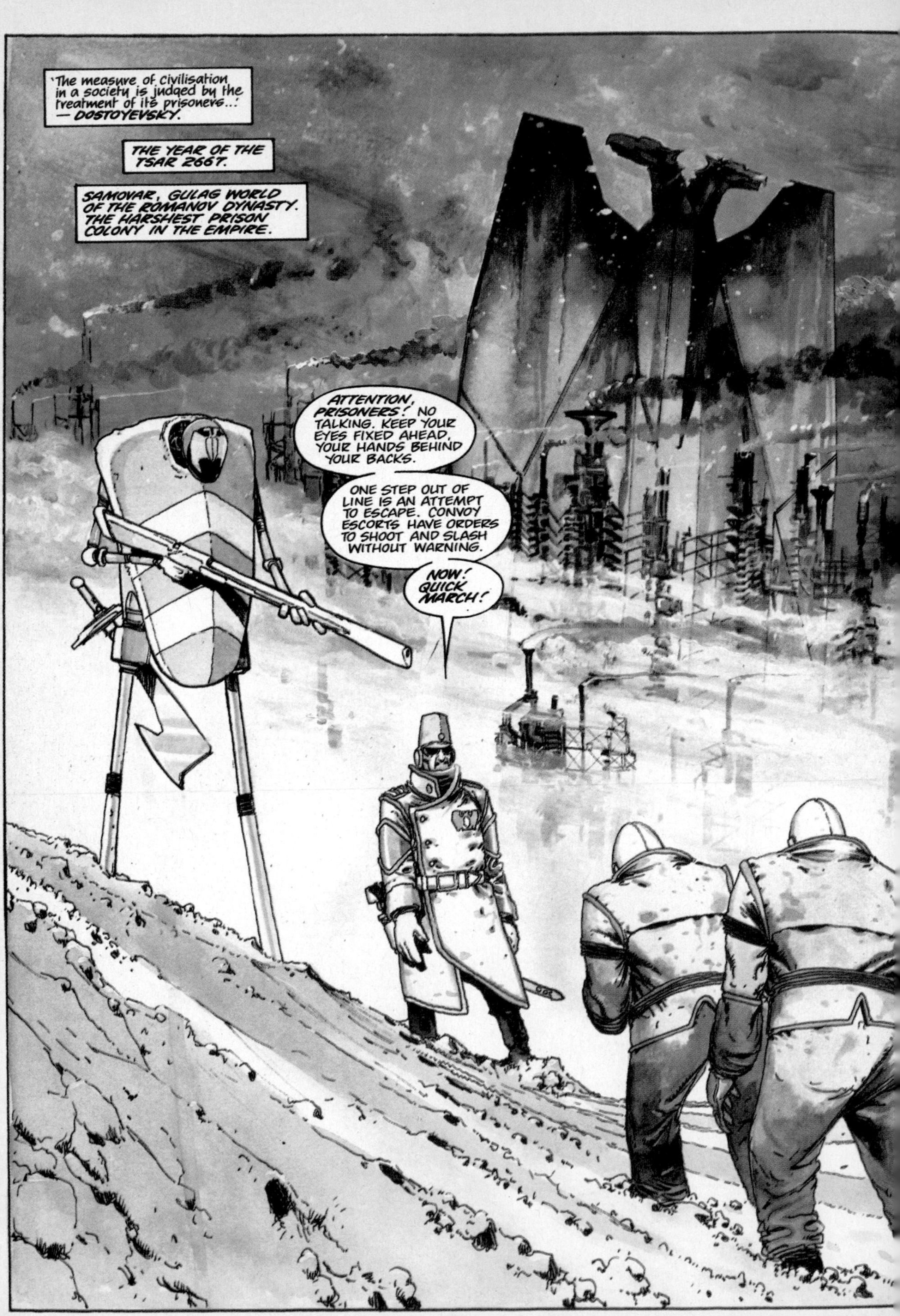

'The measure of civilisation in a society is judged by the treatment of its prisoners...' — DOSTOYEVSKY.
THE YEAR OF THE TSAR 2667.
SAMOVAR, GULAG WORLD OF THE ROMANOV DYNASTY. THE HARSHEST PRISON COLONY IN THE EMPIRE.
ATTENTION, PRISONERS! NO TALKING. KEEP YOUR EYES FIXED AHEAD, YOUR HANDS BEHIND YOUR BACKS.
ONE STEP OUT OF LINE IS AN ATTEMPT TO ESCAPE. CONVOY ESCORTS HAVE ORDERS TO SHOOT AND SLASH WITHOUT WARNING.
NOW! QUICK MARCH!

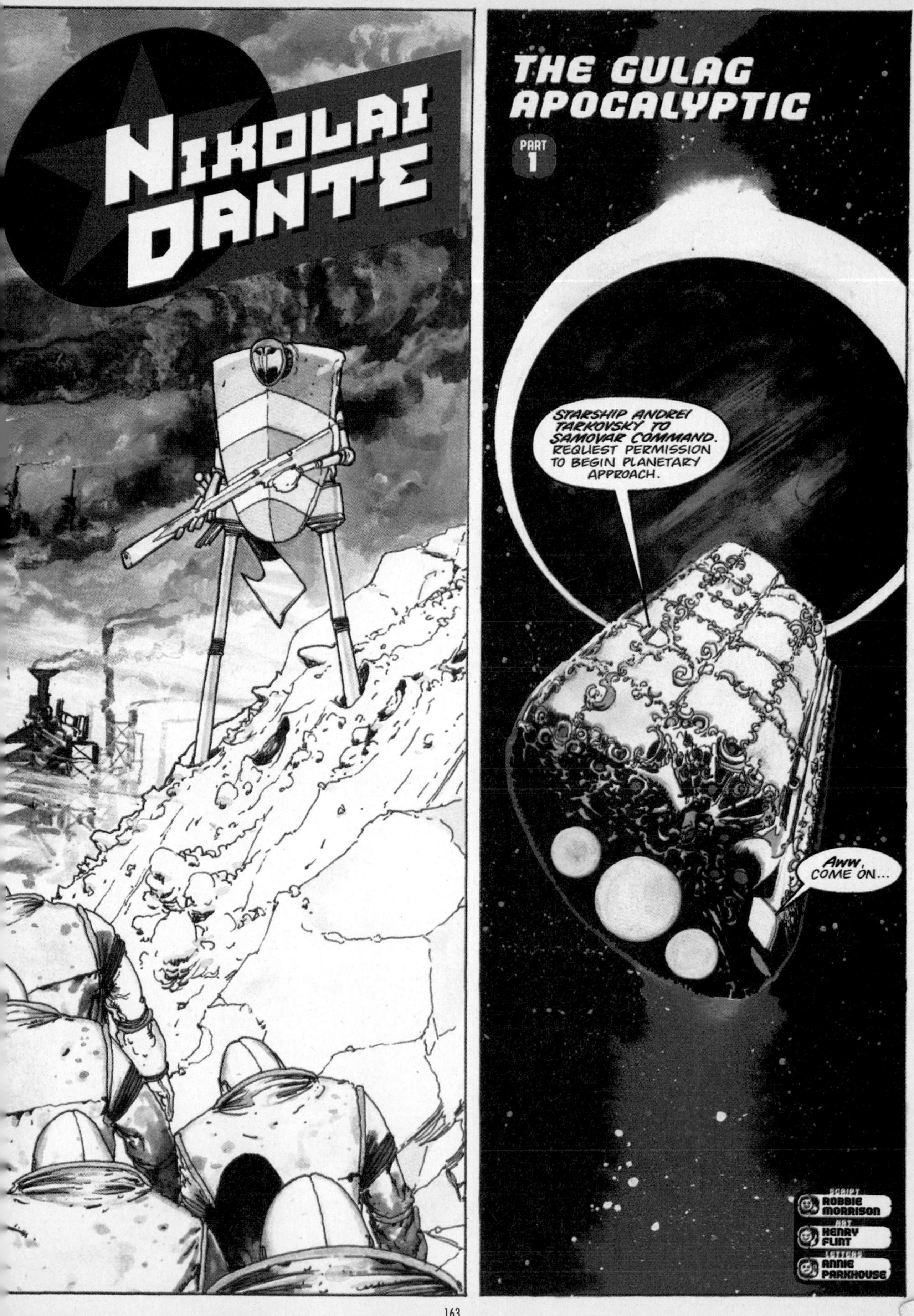
NIKOLAI DANTE
THE GULAG APOCALYPTIC
PART 1
STARSHIP ANDREI TARKOVSKY TO SAMOVAR COMMAND. REQUEST PERMISSION TO BEGIN PLANETARY APPROACH.
AWW, COME ON...
SCRIPT ROBBIE MORRISON
ART HENRY FLINT
LETTERS ANNIE PARKHOUSE

YOU *MUST* BE IMPRESSED BY NOW.

LOOK! ONE HAND!

AND IF I CAN DO THIS, JUST IMAGINE WHAT *OTHER* POSITIONS I CAN GET INTO.

COME ON, WE'RE NEARLY THERE...

AT LEAST TELL ME YOUR NAME.

KHARA.

NICE NAME...

AS GOOD AS ANY OTHER—AND OF ABSOLUTELY *NO* IMPORTANCE TO YOU.

YOU CAN *RETIRE* NOW. I'M GOING TO TAKE A SHOWER.

RETIRE!?

LADY KHARA, I TAKE MY DUTIES *VERY* SERIOUSLY. I INSIST UPON ACCOMPANYING YOU.

WHAT IF YOU *SCALD* YOURSELF, OR FAIL TO PROPERLY *LATHER UP* INTIMATE PARTS OF YOUR BODY?

MY REPUTATION AS A BODYGUARD WOULD BE IN TATTERS.

I CAN'T POSSIBLY LET YOU OUT OF MY...

SIGHTS?

STRANGE... I WAS THINKING *EXACTLY* THE SAME OF YOU.

I'LL, *UH,* MAKE SURE EVERYTHING'S SECURE BACK IN YOUR SUITE, JUST IN CASE SOMEONE ATTACKS FROM THERE.

A *WISE* STRATEGY. AND IN CASE YOU FORGET, MY RIFLE WILL BE WITHIN EASY REACH.

NAKED AND DRIPPING OR FULLY CLOTHED, I'M AN *EXCELLENT* SHOT.

'NAKED AND DRIPPING!' BOJEMOI...

CREST? *X-RAY VISION* ISN'T AMONG THE CAPABILITIES YOU CAN GIVE ME, IS IT?

NO. NOT FOR THE UNGENTLEMANLY PURPOSE YOU HAVE IN MIND.

OH, *NIKOLAI!*

AREN'T YOU SUSPICIOUS THAT YOUR ESCORTING ME MIGHT BE AN ELABORATE PLOY FOR THE ROMANOV DYNASTY TO RID THEMSELVES OF YOUR EMBARRASSING PRESENCE?

NO ONE RETURNS FROM SAMOVAR, ISN'T THAT WHAT THEY SAY?

THE WINTER PALACE OF THE ROMANOV DYNASTY, THREE DAYS AGO.

AS WELL AS BEING OUR MAIN GULAG, *SAMOVAR* IS OUR RICHEST SOURCE OF MINERALS AND FUEL.

YOU WILL ESCORT OUR VISITING ALLY HERE TO SAMOVAR COMMAND. IT'S VITAL THAT HER IDENTITY REMAINS A SECRET TO ALL CONCERNED WITH THE FLIGHT, INCLUDING YOURSELF.

WHAT YOU DON'T KNOW CAN'T HURT YOU— *OR US.*

ONCE YOU'VE DELIVERED HER SAFELY, YOU'LL REMAIN THERE, FAMILIARISING YOURSELF WITH OUR OFFWORLD HOLDINGS, UNTIL WE SEND FOR YOU.

AND WHEN WILL THAT BE?

IT'S JUST I'VE GOT A *THING* ABOUT PRISONS, *LORD DMITRI*— EVERY WOMAN I'VE EVER KNOWN TOLD ME I'D END UP IN ONE.

'FACT. MOST OF THEM SAID THEY'D HAPPILY DO THE *LOCKING UP.*

IT'LL BE WHEN WE SEND FOR YOU.

AND I LIKE IT HERE AT THE PALACE.

I MEAN. IT'LL BE *COLD* WAY OUT THERE.

OH, POOR BOY...

DON'T WORRY. I'LL BUY YOU A *GREATCOAT.*

THE STARSHIP ANDREI TARKOVSKY. NOW.

A GREATCOAT...

GREAT.

BEGINNING FINAL DESCENT, SAMOVAR COMMAND. PLEASE RESPOND.

LORD DANTE! SENSORS ARE REGISTERING SOME KIND OF ENERGY SURGE FROM THE CENTRAL CORE OF THE GULAG...

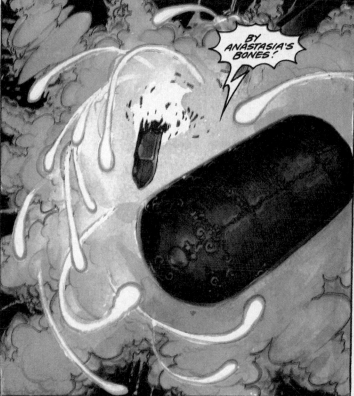

BY ANASTASIA'S BONES!

FUOCO!

LOOKS LIKE OUR FINAL DESCENT MIGHT BE A WEE BIT MORE FINAL THAN I'D LIKE!

NEXT PROG ▷ COMPROMISING POSITIONS!

'When it comes to being in the wrong place at the wrong time, there's not a man alive can touch me.'

'The explosion that disabled the Samovar prison colony brought down our ship, killing the crew.'
— NIKOLAI DANTE, BRIEFING THE ROMANOV DYNASTY ON THE SAMOVAR INCIDENT.

NIKOLAI DANTE

PART 2 THE GULAG APOCALYPTIC

SCRIPT
ROBBIE MORRISON

ART
HENRY FLINT

LETTERS
ANNIE PARKHOUSE

'Luckily, I had a soft landing.'

nuhhh...

WHAT!? HUH?

TALK ABOUT COMPROMISING POSITIONS.

HOPE YOU DON'T THINK I ENGINEERED THE CRASH JUST TO SET THIS UP?

NO, NIKOLAI.

I WOULDN'T CREDIT YOU WITH THAT MUCH INTELLIGENCE.

CREW OF THE ANDREI TARKOVSKY!

LAY DOWN YOUR WEAPONS AND SURRENDER YOURSELVES IN THE NAME OF THE ROMANOV DYNASTY!

WHO!?

THE *ISOLATORS*. THE GULAG'S ANDROID ENFORCERS.

MAYBE YOU SHOULD IDENTIFY YOURSELF BEFORE THEY RECOGNISE YOUR CRIMINAL TENDENCIES AND MISTAKE YOU FOR A NEW ARRIVAL.

THE NAME'S *DANTE*. *NIKOLAI DANTE*.

AS FAR AS YOU'RE CONCERNED, I *AM* THE ROMANOV DYNASTY, SO START SHOWING SOME RESPECT OR I'LL ISOLATE YOUR HEAD FROM YOUR BODY.

WAS THAT *DOMINANT* ENOUGH FOR YOU?

Dante! The Isolators aren't responding to my communications!

WHOA! CREST!?

An unidentified intelligence has infiltrated their command network —they are no longer under Romanov control!

SLASH

SHXXX!

KHARA!

GET OUT OF HERE! I'LL TAKE CARE OF THEM!

My nevo...

KRZZ-KK-K!

CREST, YOU'RE THE *SUPER-COOL* BATTLE COMPUTER. *DO* SOMETHING!

REGAIN CONTROL OR BLAST THEIR CIRCUITS TO KINGDOM COME!

Don't you think I'm trying?

TRY HARDER!!

BDAMM!

BDAMM!

BDAMM!

BDAMM!

NICE MOVE, CREST.

I HAD *EVERY* CONFIDENCE IN YOUR ABILITIES.

Unlike you, Dante, I cannot tell a lie — I had nothing to do with their destruction.

WITH *RESPECT,* NIKOLAI...

YOU'RE SUPPOSED TO BE *MY* BODYGUARD?

WE'LL HEAD FOR *SAMOVAR COMMAND* —WHAT'S *LEFT* OF IT—AND HAVE YOUR WEAPONS CREST ANALYSE THE SITUATION.

SURE THING— AFTER SEEING YOUR SHOOTING, I'M NOT GOING TO ARGUE.

QUITE A PISTOL YOU'RE PACKING.

THE *HUNTSMAN 5000* A SELF-RELIANT, MULTI-PURPOSE WEAPONS SYSTEM, CODED SPECIFICALLY TO MY *GENEPRINT.*

AMMUNITION IS CREATED INTERNALLY AND REPLENISHED AUTOMATICALLY— NO NEED TO LOAD OR RELOAD.

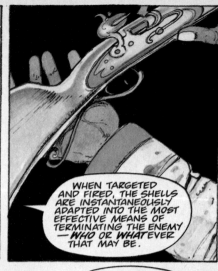

WHEN TARGETED AND FIRED, THE SHELLS ARE INSTANTANEOUSLY ADAPTED INTO THE MOST EFFECTIVE MEANS OF TERMINATING THE ENEMY —*WHO* OR *WHAT*EVER THAT MAY BE.

IT'S THE *FINEST* WEAPON I'VE EVER KNOWN.

HANDLE IT WITH CARE AND RESPECT.

'COURSE!

WONDERFUL DESIGN. YOUR EYES JUST *FLOW* TOWARDS THE *TARGET.*

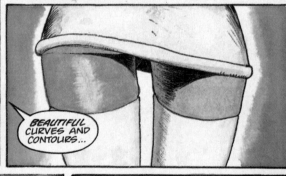

BEAUTIFUL CURVES AND CONTOURS...

WHAT?

NOTHING! PICK A TARGET AND I'LL SHOW YOU HOW ACCURATELY I *SHOOT MY LOAD.*

I'D *LOVE* TO SEE YOU TRY.

IT'S CODED TO MY *GENEPRINT*—IF ANYONE ELSE FIRES IT, THE BULLET REVERSES TRAJECTORY AND USES THEM FOR *TARGET PRACTICE.*

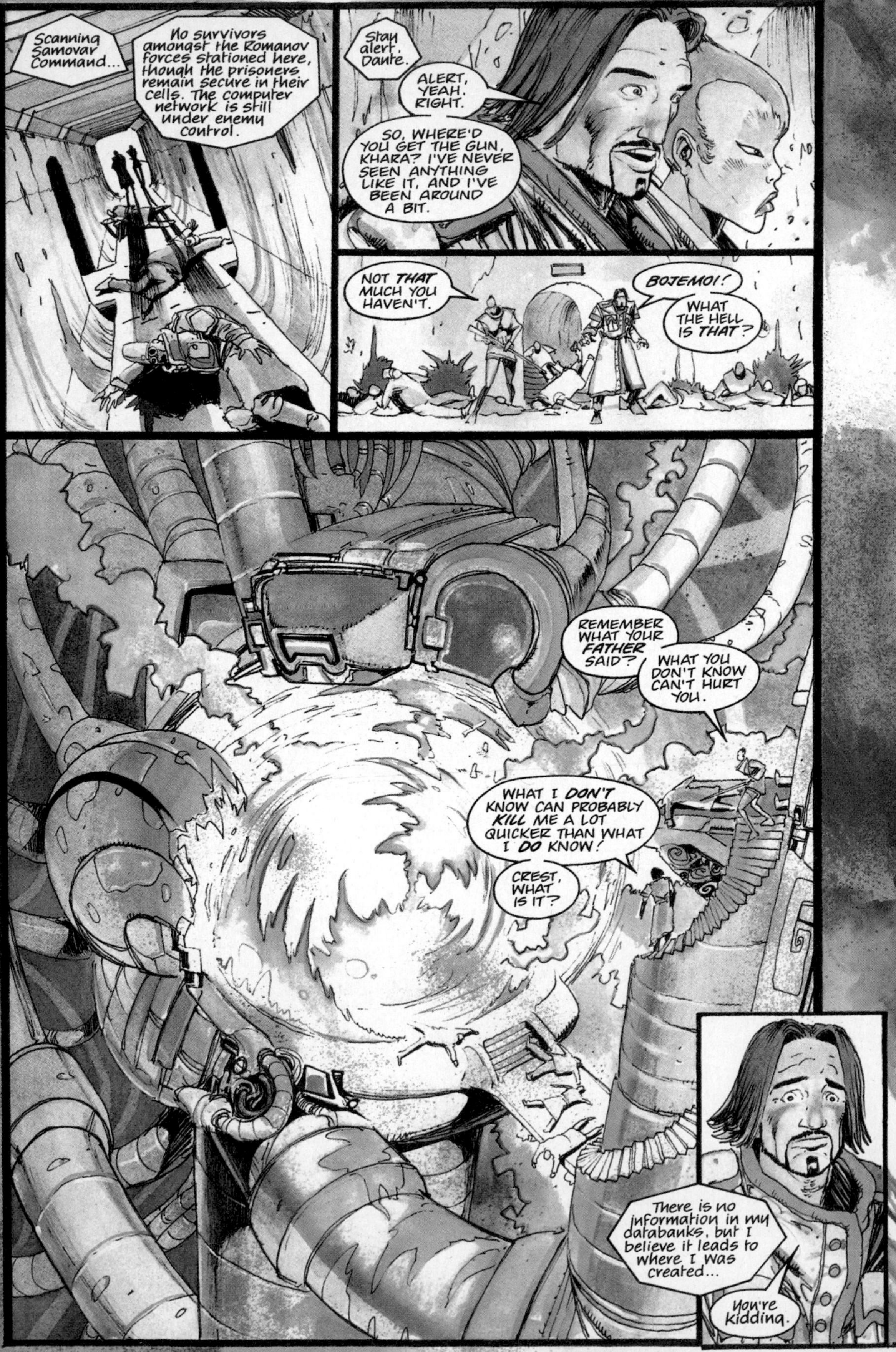
Scanning Samovar Command...
No survivors amongst the Romanov forces stationed here, though the prisoners remain secure in their cells. The computer network is still under enemy control.
Stay alert, Dante.
ALERT, YEAH. RIGHT.
SO, WHERE'D YOU GET THE GUN, KHARA? I'VE NEVER SEEN ANYTHING LIKE IT, AND I'VE BEEN AROUND A BIT.
NOT THAT MUCH YOU HAVEN'T.
BOJEMOI!
WHAT THE HELL IS THAT?
REMEMBER WHAT YOUR FATHER SAID?
WHAT YOU DON'T KNOW CAN'T HURT YOU.
WHAT I DON'T KNOW CAN PROBABLY KILL ME A LOT QUICKER THAN WHAT I DO KNOW!
CREST, WHAT IS IT?
There is no information in my databanks, but I believe it leads to where I was created...
You're kidding.

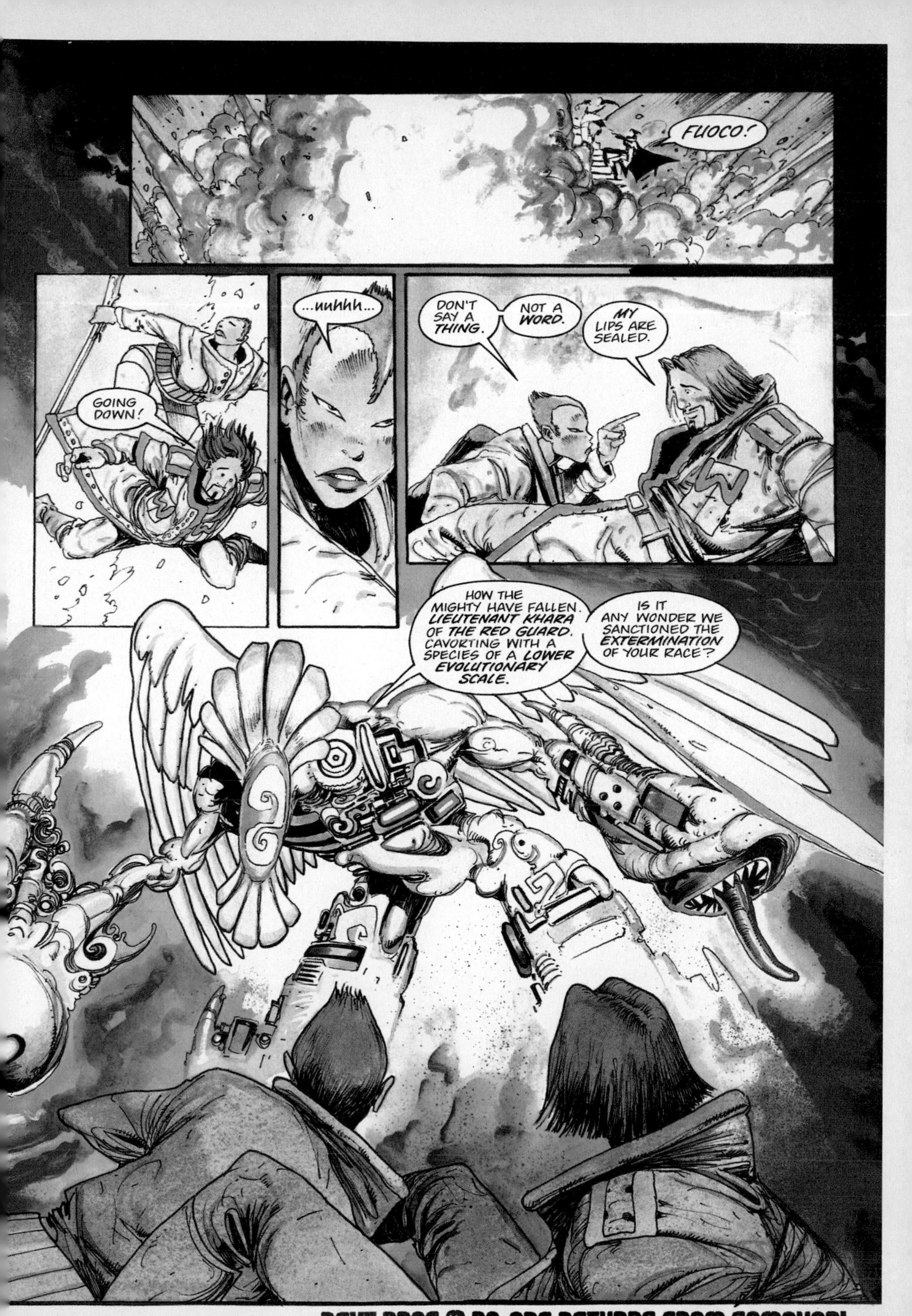
FUOCO!
GOING DOWN!
...uuhhh...
DON'T SAY A THING.
NOT A WORD.
MY LIPS ARE SEALED.
HOW THE MIGHTY HAVE FALLEN. LIEUTENANT KHARA OF THE RED GUARD, CAVORTING WITH A SPECIES OF A LOWER EVOLUTIONARY SCALE.
IS IT ANY WONDER WE SANCTIONED THE EXTERMINATION OF YOUR RACE?

NEXT PROG ⏩ NO-ONE RETURNS FROM SAMOVAR!

'Under attack from an enemy who had singlehandedly seized control of the Samovar prison colony and decimated the troops stationed there...

'I defended myself and the lovely Lady Khara with the courage and determination one would expect from the Hero of Rudinshtein.'

NIKOLAI DANTE, EMBELLISHING HIS ROLE IN THE SAMOVAR INCIDENT TO THE ROMANOV DYNASTY.

NIKOLAI DANTE

THE GULAG APOCALYPTIC
PART 3

SCRIPT
ROBBIE MORRISON

ART
HENRY FLINT

LETTERS
ANNIE PARKHOUSE

YOUR CHOICE IS *SIMPLE*, KHARA. BECOME *ONE* WITH US.

OR *DIE*.

THE LADY'S UNDER MY PROTECTION.

YOU WANT *HER*, YOU HAVE TO CROSS BLADES WITH *ME*...

AS YOU WISH, *ANIMAL*.

Dante--

I KNOW, I KNOW...

EVASIVE ACTION!

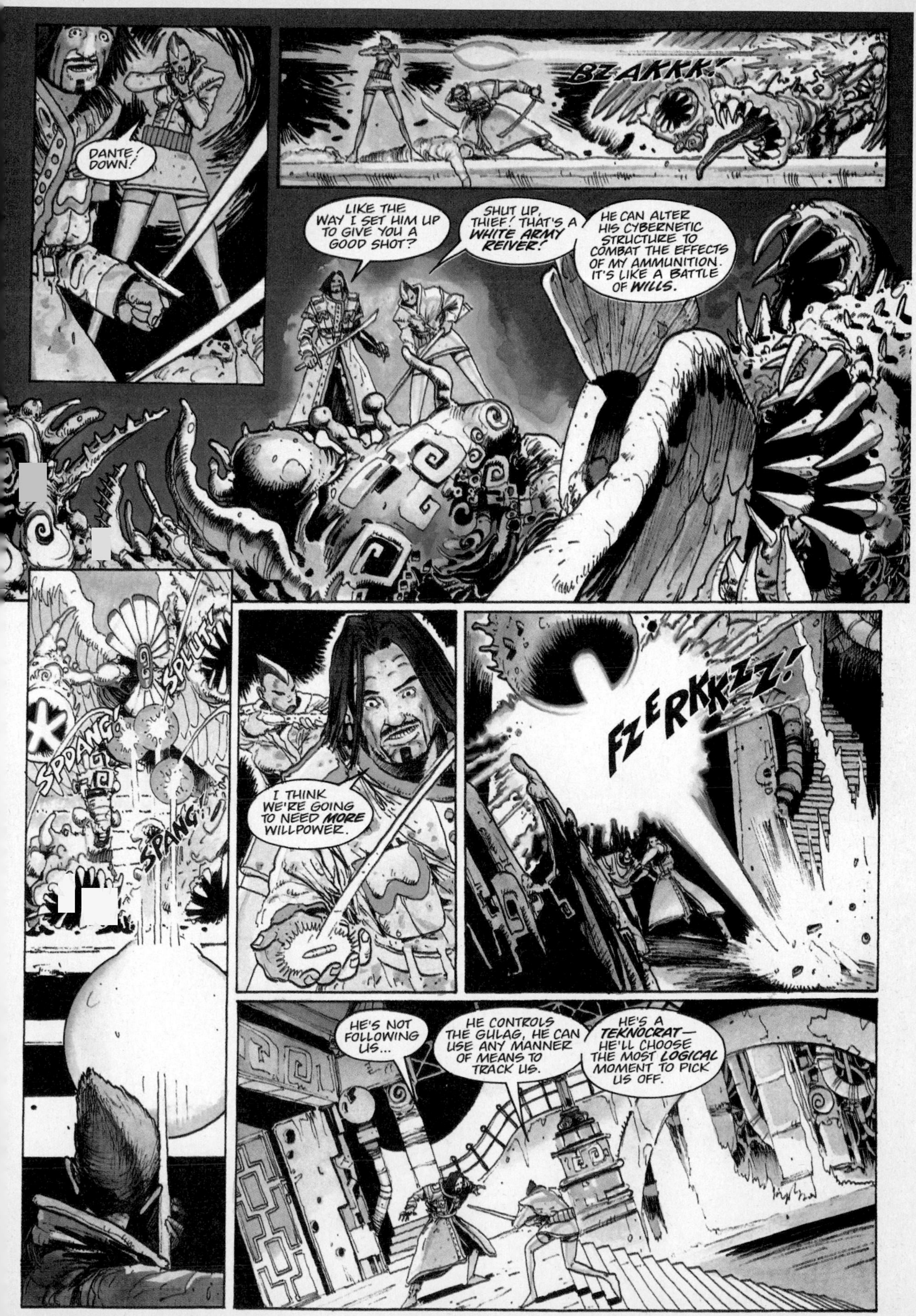
DANTE! DOWN!
BZAKKK!
LIKE THE WAY I SET HIM UP TO GIVE YOU A GOOD SHOT?
SHUT UP, THIEF! THAT'S A WHITE ARMY REIVER!
HE CAN ALTER HIS CYBERNETIC STRUCTURE TO COMBAT THE EFFECTS OF MY AMMUNITION. IT'S LIKE A BATTLE OF WILLS.
SPLUT!
SPDANG!
SPANG!
I THINK WE'RE GOING TO NEED MORE WILLPOWER.
FZERKKZZ!
HE'S NOT FOLLOWING US...
HE CONTROLS THE GULAG, HE CAN USE ANY MANNER OF MEANS TO TRACK US.
HE'S A TEKNOCRAT— HE'LL CHOOSE THE MOST LOGICAL MOMENT TO PICK US OFF.

YOU DESERVE TO KNOW THE TRUTH, NIKOLAI, EVEN IF YOU *HATE* US ALL FOR IT.

'DECADES AGO, CYBORGANIC TECHNOLOGY SIMILAR TO YOUR WEAPONS CREST WAS INTRODUCED TO MY RACE, TO FURTHER OUR EVOLUTION, TO *IMPROVE* US, BUT TECHNOLOGY DOESN'T WORK THAT WAY...

'ITS PURPOSE IS TO *ADVANCE ITSELF* — AT ANY PRICE. IT BEGAN TRANSFORMING US INTO LIFEFORMS LIKE THE REIVER, MORE CYBERNETIC THAN ORGANIC.

'OUR SOCIETY SPLIT INTO TWO FACTIONS: *THE WHITE ARMY,* WHICH EMBRACES THE MUTATIONAL PROCESS AND HAS SWORN TO WIPE OUT THE WEAKNESSES OF THE FLESH; AND *THE RED GUARD,* WHO FIGHT TO PRESERVE OUR 'HUMANITY':

'THE ENERGY VORTEX YOU SAW IS A **BRIDGE** BETWEEN MY UNIVERSE AND YOURS, CAUSED BY SOME COSMIC UPHEAVAL. THE REIVER MUST HAVE INFILTRATED THE FORTRESS WE BUILT AROUND IT.

'THROUGH THE BRIDGE, THE RED GUARD AND THE ROMANOV DYNASTY FORMED AN ALLIANCE. IN RETURN FOR CREST TECHNOLOGY, THE ROMANOVS SUPPLY US WITH **UNTAINTED GENETIC MATERIAL** TO COMBAT THE ONSLAUGHT OF CYBORGANIC MUTATION.

'*GULAG INMATES* WHO HAVE GROWN TOO WEAK TO WORK SAMOVAR ANY LONGER!'

No one returns from Samovar...

SAMOVAR OIL PRODUCTION PLATFORMS.

NOT THE CLEVEREST PLACE FOR US TO BE — A FIREFIGHT'LL TURN THE PLATFORM INTO AN INFERNO.

US!? NICE TO KNOW YOU'RE CONCERNED ABOUT A PIECE OF GENETIC MATERIAL LIKE ME!

THE INMATES SENT TO US WERE MURDERERS, RAPISTS--

THE REIVER MUST'VE BROKEN THE PRODUCTION PROGRAMME WHEN HE COMMANDEERED SAMOVAR'S COMPUTER NETWORK.

THE WELLS ARE LEAKING BADLY.

YEAH, YEAH! AND THIEVES WHO STOLE TO FEED THEIR FAMILIES, DISSIDENTS STUPID ENOUGH TO THINK THEY COULD CHANGE THE EMPIRE JUST BY TALKING ABOUT IT AND ANY OTHER POOR SCUMBAG WHO WASN'T COOL ENOUGH TO BE BORN INTO THE ARISTOCRACY.

MY KIND OF PEOPLE!

WHAT KIND ARE YOU!?

I'M A WAR-CHILD, WHAT THE WHITE ARMY MADE ME! I'LL DO WHATEVER I HAVE TO TO FIGHT THEM!

I DON'T HAVE TO BE PROUD OF IT!

I HOPE YOU NEVER TASTE WAR, NIKOLAI. IT'S ALL I'VE EVER KNOWN.

NOTHING'S BLACK AND WHITE.

IT'S NEVER THAT EASY...

IT CAN BE, LIEUTENANT KHARA. YOU ONLY HAVE TO BECOME ONE WITH US.

178

EVERYTHING IS SIMPLE WHEN YOU ELIMINATE THE *FRAILTY* OF THE FLESH, THE *WEAKNESS* OF THE MIND.

THE DOUBTS, THE DESIRES, THE VICES, THE EMOTIONS.

I'M ALL FOR VICES.

THE *BIGGER* THE *BETTER*.

YOU BELIEVE YOURSELF SUPERIOR TO ME FOR ALL THE REASONS I KNOW YOU TO BE *INFERIOR*.

IF EMOTION EXISTED WITHIN ME, I WOULD *RELISH* KILLING YOU, *ANIMAL*.

I'M TOO *COOL* TO *KILL*.

KA-BOOOMM!

NEXT PROG ▷ BIG BANG BOOM!

YOU WILL BE ONE OF US, LIEUTENANT KHARA!

UUUNNHH!

THE WHITE ARMY *WELCOMES* YOU INTO ITS RANKS.

NO...

REIVER!

THE LADY'S UNDER *MY* PROTECTION.

YOU STILL WISH TO *CROSS SWORDS* WITH ME, ANIMAL?

YEAH! CROSS THEM AND *SHOVE THEM UP* YOUR --

AAAGHKK!

I WILL CRUSH YOU, *ANIMAL*, CRUSH *ALL* YOUR KIND.

YOU *CAN'T* CRUSH US ANY FURTHER, REIVER.

YOU, THE *ROMANOVS*, THE *TSAR*, YOU'RE ALL THE SAME.

I'M GOING TO RAISE A *SEWER*-BRED ARMY OF *THIEVES*, *SEDUCTRESSES* AND *MURDERERS*.

WE'LL *FIGHT* AND *BOOZE* AND *SLEEP* OUR WAY ACROSS THE UNIVERSE, BRING DOWN *YOUR* EMPIRE, THIS EMPIRE...

EVERY EMPIRE.

WE'LL CRUSH YOU INTO THE GUTTER, GIVE YOU A TASTE OF *REALITY*.

WE'LL RULE OVER YOU, SEE WHO'S *WORSE*...

OR IF WE'RE *ALL* AS BAD AS EACH OTHER.

YOUR WORDS ARE BORN OF INSANITY, BUT YOU *FENCE* WELL, IF NOTHING ELSE.

I HAD A *GOOD* TEACHER.

BEST IN THE EMPIRE.

THERE IS MORE TO WAR THAN FENCING, *ANIMAL SCUM*!!

THE NAME'S DANTE! NIKOLAI DANTE!

PRIZE SCUMBAG OF THE RUSSIAN EMPIRE!

BEEEEEAAGH!

AND PROUD OF IT...

YOU KILLED HIM?

A WHITE ARMY REIVER, NIKOLAI? AND YOU KILLED HIM?

I TOLD YOU, LADY KHARA, I TAKE MY DUTIES AS A BODYGUARD VERY SERIOUSLY.

SPEAKING OF BODIES, WE BETTER GET SOME SHELTER BEFORE OURS START FREEZING.

OHH, I'M SURE YOU'LL THINK UP SOME WAY OF KEEPING US WARM...

YOU HUMANS ARE SO *POORLY* EVOLVED.

ALL *HAIRY* AND *UGLY.*

HEY, A BIT OF *ROUGH* NEVER HURT ANYBODY.

YOUR REINFORCEMENTS ARE ARRIVING.

I HAVE TO GO. *I'M SORRY...*

A *GREATCOAT.* *GREAT.*

THE BRIDGE WILL RETURN ME TO MY PEOPLE. I'VE REPROGRAMMED THE *HUNTSMAN* TO ENCODE ITSELF TO YOU. YOUR GENE-PRINT WILL AUTOMATICALLY SUPERSEDE MINE.

KEEP IT...

YOU NEED *EVERYTHING* YOU CAN TO HELP YOU STAY ALIVE.

STAY WITH ME...

KOLYA...

IT'S NOT AS IF WE'RE ONLY FROM DIFFERENT WORLDS OR *GALAXIES —* WE'RE FROM *DIFFERENT DIMENSIONS.*

SO?

YOU'RE A *FOOL*, NIKOLAI DANTE.

YEAH...

AN *UGLY* FOOL AT THAT.

OUR ORDERS ARE TO IMPOSE ORDER ONCE MORE AND RETURN YOU TO THE WINTER PALACE WITH ALL POSSIBLE HASTE.

ANY ADVICE ON PLANETARY CONDITIONS, LORD NIKOLAI?

ADVICE? SURE...

DON'T EAT ANY YELLOW SNOW.

2000 AD Prog 1035: Cover by **Simon Davis**

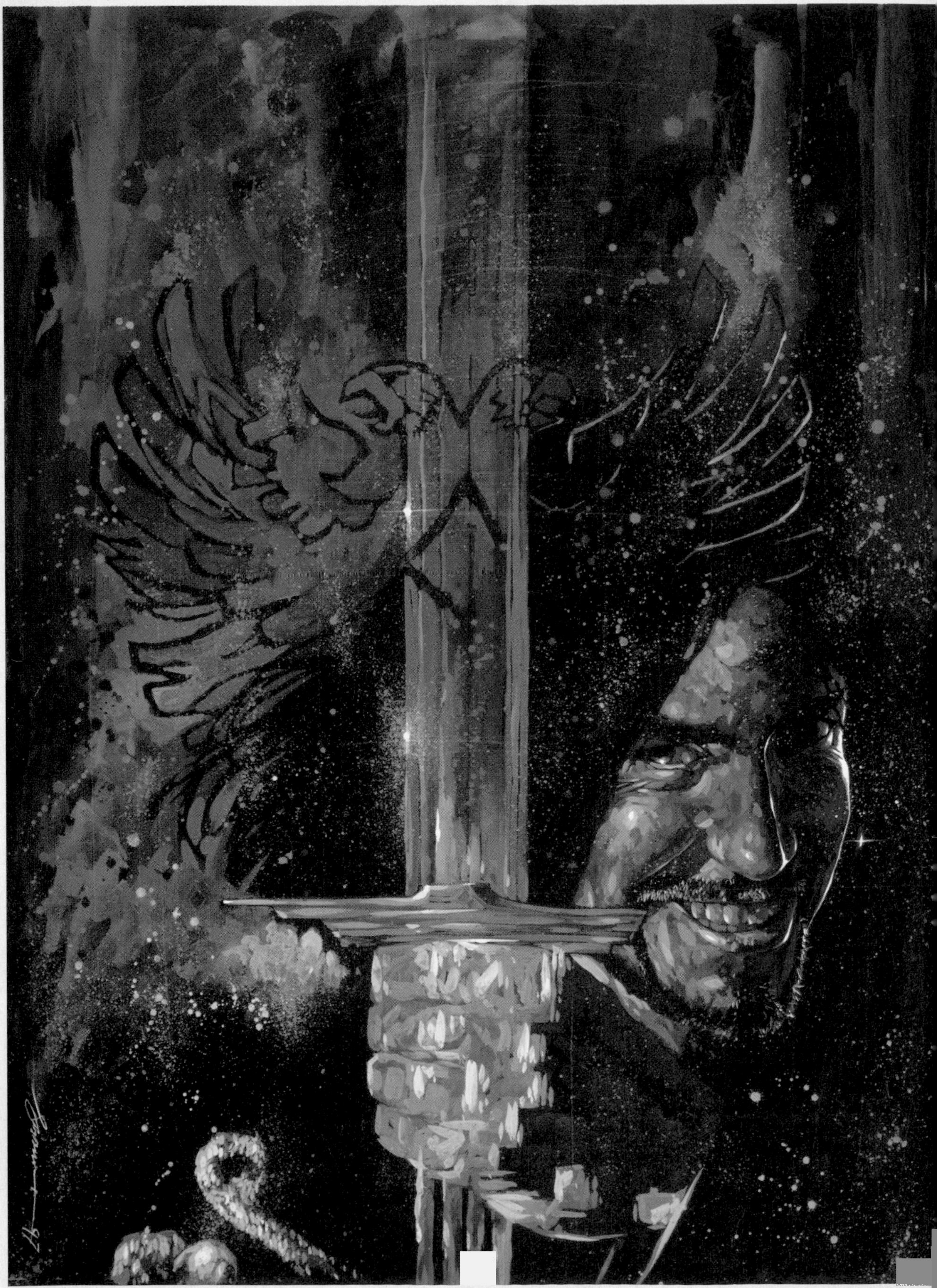

2000 AD Prog 1039: Cover by **Simon Davis**

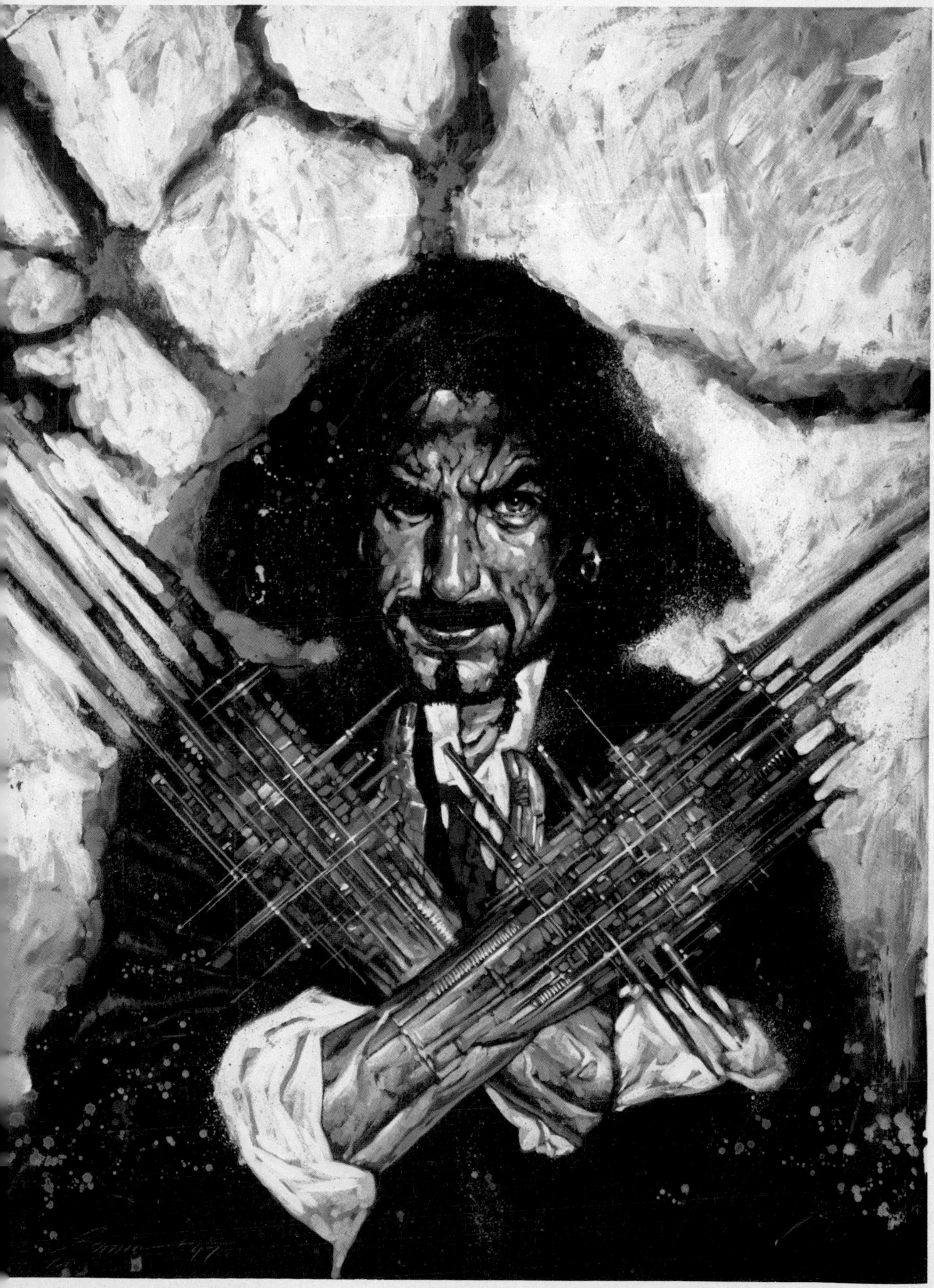

2000 AD Prog 1044: Cover by **Trevor Hairsine**

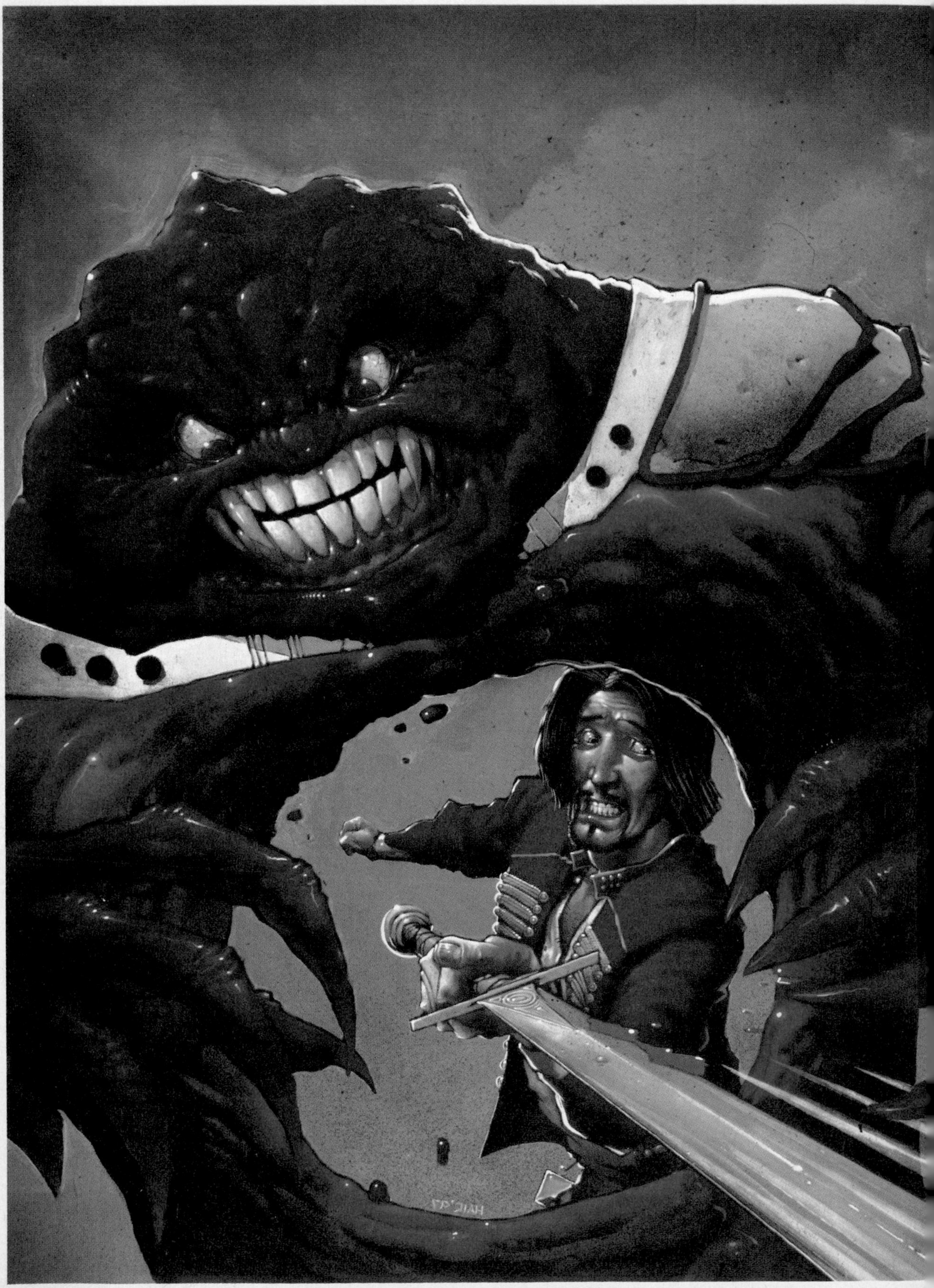

2000 AD Prog 1074: Cover by **Trevor Hairsine**

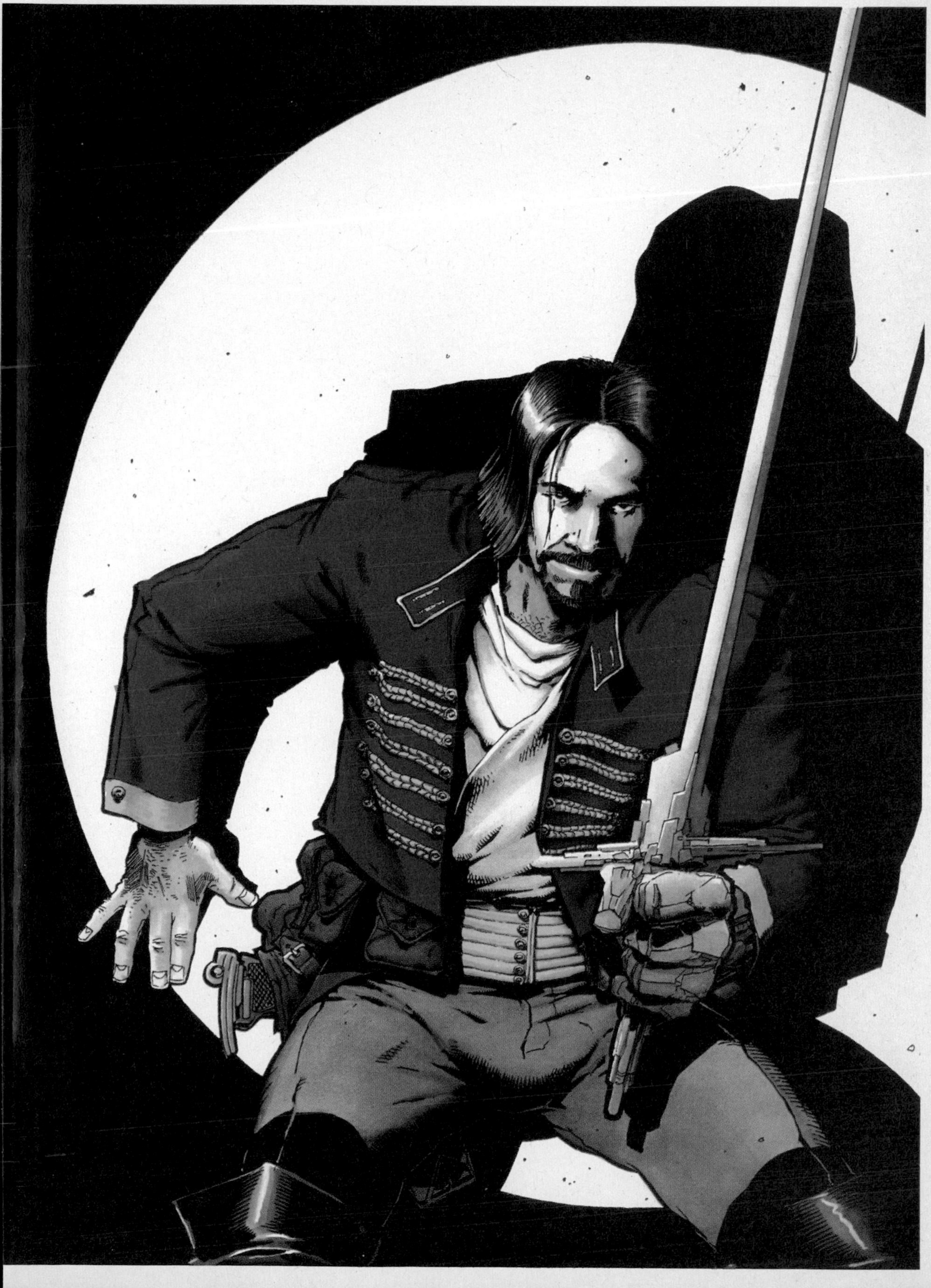

2000 AD Prog 1080: Cover by **Henry Flint**

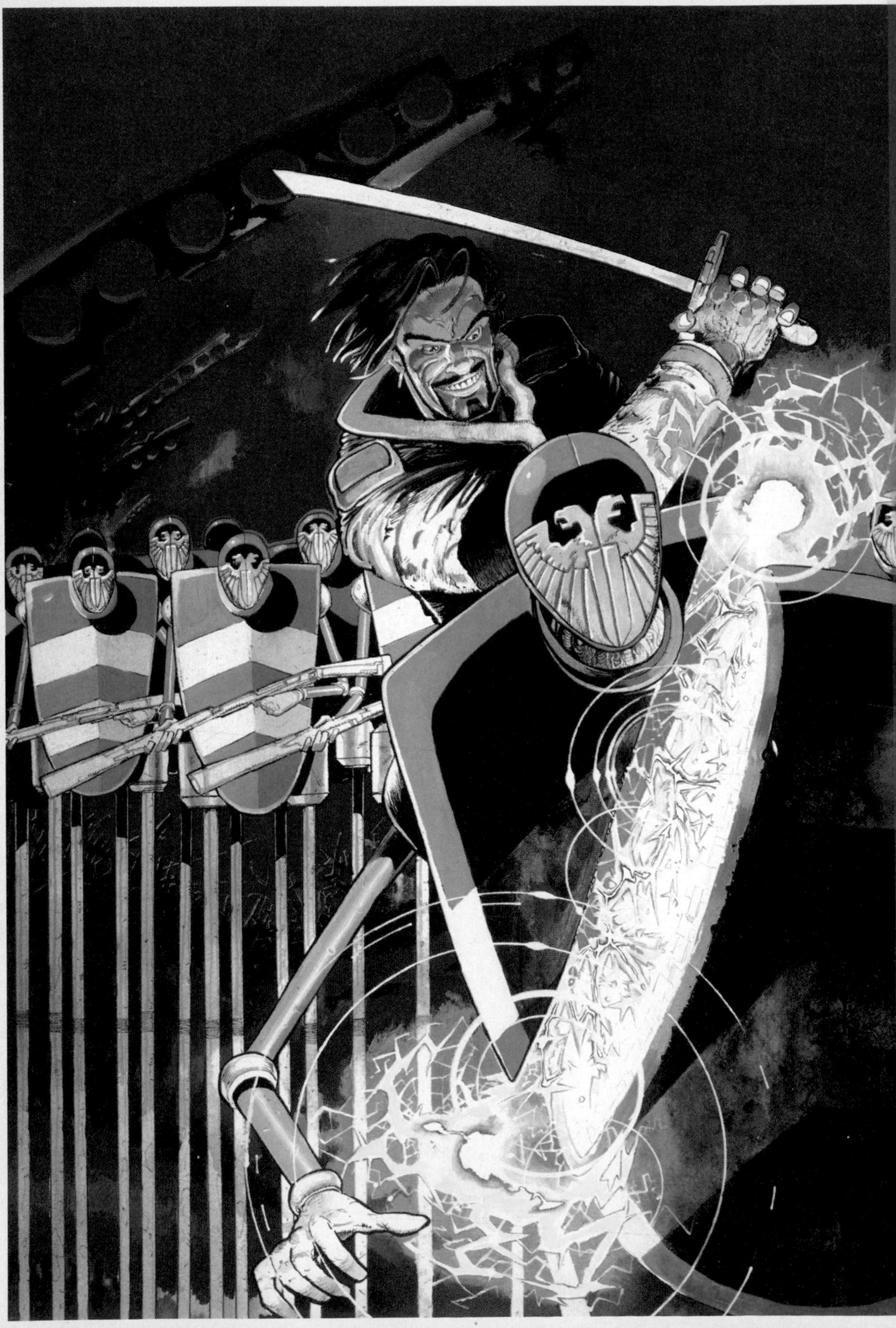

Nikolai Dante portrait
by **Simon Fraser**

Early Jena Makarov sketch
by **Simon Fraser**

Robbie Morrison is one of *2000 AD*'s most popular writers, having co-created *Blackheart*, *The Bendatti Vendetta*, *Shakara*, *Shimura* and *Vanguard*, and chronicled the adventures of Judge Dredd in *2000 AD*, *Judge Dredd Megazine* and a UK national newspaper. He is also co-creator of the fan-favorite Russian rogue *Nikolai Dante*, which recently won an Eagle award for Best UK Character — beating Judge Dredd to this accolade for the first time in almost twenty years.

In the US, Morrison has written *Spider-Man's Tangled Web* for Marvel and recently completed work on a new story arc for DC/WildStorm's *The Authority*. His critically acclaimed graphic novel *White Death* has been hugely successful in both Europe and the US, and he and *White Death* artist Charlie Adlard have recently reunited for a story in DC's *Batman*.

Charlie Adlard made his debut pencilling *Judge Dredd* in the eponymous *Magazine*. Since then, he has also illustrated *Armitage* and *Judge Hershey* in the *Meg*, and *Judge Dredd*, *Nikolai Dante*, *Pulp Sci-Fi* and *Rogue Trooper* in *2000 AD*. His most recent work for the Galaxy's Greatest Comic is the official sequel to *Invasion!*, the hard-hitting *Savage*. Beyond *2000 AD*, Adlard has illustrated *Astronauts in Trouble*, *Codeflesh*, *The Establishment*, *Shadowman*, *The X-Files*, and the graphic novel *White Death*.

Simon Fraser is best known to *2000 AD* fans as the co-creator of Russian rogue Nikolai Dante, whose adventures have been a staple of the comic since his debut in 1997. Fraser is also the co-creator of *Family* in the *Judge Dredd Megazine*, and he has drawn *Judge Dredd* and *Shimura* as well. His best-known non-*2000 AD* work is *Lux & Alby: Sign On and Save the Universe*, a collaboration with Scottish post-punk author Martin Millar. Fraser is currently working on an adaptation of Richard Matheson's *Hell House* and is also writing and drawing *Lilly Mackenzie and the Mines of Charybdis*.

Henry Flint is one of the Galaxy's Greatest Comic's rising superstars. Co-creator of *Sancho Panzer* and *Shakara*, he has also lent his incredibly versatile pencils to *A.B.C. Warriors*, *Judge Dredd/Aliens*, *Bill Savage*, *Deadlock*, *Judge Dredd*, *Rogue Trooper*, *Missionary Man*, *Nemesis the Warlock*, *Nikolai Dante*, *Sinister Dexter*, *Tharg the Mighty*, *The V.C.s*, *Vector 13* and *Venus Bluegenes*. He has even written a *Tharg's Alien Invasions* strip! In addition, Flint has begun to establish himself in American comics, working on the anthology titles *AIDS Awareness*, *Ammo Armageddon* and *Monster Massacre*.